A Journey for Leah

SARAH LAMB

Contents

Dedication

For those who have to make a journey of any sort, without knowing what will happen.

Chapter 1

Independence, Missouri 1845

Leah Dearing smiled as she looked at the note shoved under her boarding room door. How Jim had gotten past her strict landlady she'd never know, but somehow he had.

Meet me at our spot as soon as you see this. I've got something to tell you.

Her heart beat quickly. What was it he wanted to tell her? Jim was always prone to secrecy. In fact, their entire relationship had been kept that way, much to her dismay. She wasn't sure why. Mrs. Smith, the boarding house owner, wouldn't have cared if she had a gentleman caller, so long as he wasn't in her room. They could have sat in the parlor together. He could have walked her home from work. So far, he hadn't done any of those things. Usually, their meetings were short, in a quiet area, or at night.

It made Leah feel a little sad, but at least she had someone interested in her, she was fond of reminding herself. Unlike so many women who had to get a marriage of convenience or even become mail-order brides, with no idea of what they were getting themselves into. No, hers might be a dull relationship, one in just fits and starts, but at least she had one. It was something, and something was better than nothing. It might grow, as well.

She hoped.

Leah read the note again, then put it into her pocket. It said right away, so that's what she should do. She didn't want to keep him waiting. Quickly, she splashed some water on her face to freshen up and smoothed her hair with her damp hands. It had been a long day at the post office. The mail wagon had come with an abundance of letters and the postmaster was home sick. It had been a little more than she could handle at times, between helping customers and sorting letters, but she'd managed.

Truthfully, had Jim not wanted to see her, she might have skipped dinner in favor of her bed she was so tired. A yawn escaped, and she knew that tomorrow promised to be just as tiring of a day, and wondered how long she and Jim would meet.

Satisfied with her appearance, Leah went back down the stairs of the boarding house. She could smell dinner cooking, and it made her stomach growl. Hopefully, she'd make it in time for the meal. Quietly, she slipped through the front door and down the street, to make her way toward the stream that was near the edge of town. There, Jim would be waiting, by their tree.

He'd even carved a heart into the trunk, and told her it was a sign of their love. She wished he'd put their initials inside of it, but he hadn't, and had gotten upset when she asked him to, so she never said anything again about it. Still, each time she saw the heart, her stomach sank just a little bit. Why, with a plain heart like that, it could belong to anyone. Not her and Jim specifically.

A loud shout and then the roar of laughter from a huge clearing caught her attention and Leah paused. There was a wagon train about to leave. Heading to Oregon, she understood. About a dozen covered wagons rested, while people milled around getting supplies gathered and stored. She wondered what it would be like to go out to Oregon. One woman from the wagon train posting a letter, a Mrs. Dunlop, had told her that out west, even women could own land. The idea wasn't unappealing, but it also seemed hard. She was grateful for her job at the post office and the room at the boarding house.

If only she had a ring on her finger and a date for the wedding, she'd be quite happy. At twenty-two, she'd be a spinster soon if that didn't happen. Who would want her then?

Picking her skirts up to walk a little faster, Leah rounded the last building in the town, the schoolhouse, and smiled when she saw Jim. He was sitting on the grass and looked up as she came closer.

"Hello, Jim," she said, her voice a little breathless.

"Hello, Leah," he said, and stood. "I'm glad you're here. Took you long enough. I've been waiting an hour."

"I'm sorry," she answered, instantly feeling guilty. "I only just saw your note. It was a busy day and—"

"Don't matter," Jim answered, and crossed his arms. He frowned then. "Why'd you wear that dress? I don't like you in yellow. You know that."

"I..." Leah's thoughts swirled. Why had she? She knew he didn't like it. He also didn't like her in green. Usually she was mindful of that, but if she wore her lavender or blue dresses every day, they'd wear out so quickly. Her cheeks heated as she tried to come up with an answer. "I'm behind on my laundry," she finally said.

He didn't answer for a long moment, then finally shrugged. "Just don't do it again. Throw that one away. You look ugly in yellow."

Leah sucked in a breath. She was used to Jim's blunt words, but that was downright hurtful. She swallowed hard and nodded, a strand of her honey-colored hair falling alongside her cheek.

"Aww, don't look so sad," Jim said, and came over to her. He raised her chin. "I didn't mean you're ugly. Just the dress."

Leah managed a smile and nodded. Jim's rough hand scratched at her cheek, but she didn't mind. He was one of the best looking men she'd ever seen. His hair was so dark it looked like the color of a raven, and he had a thin mustache he kept trimmed, along with the deepest gray eyes she'd ever seen.

"What was it you wanted to tell me?" she asked, hoping to change the topic away from her dress.

Jim dropped his hand and stepped away. "I'm leaving town for a while," he said, hooking his thumbs at his waist. "Had an opportunity."

"Oh?" She tried to ignore the worry in her stomach. "Will you be gone long?"

"That depends on you," he answered.

"On me?"

"Yes. I need some money. If you give me yours, I can hurry back faster. Otherwise, I'll have to stay away while I make some."

Leah lowered her head. "I see. How much do you need?"

"Twenty dollars will do for right now," he said, as her head shot up. "You can wire me a hundred more."

"I don't have that kind of money," Leah gasped.

"Sure you do," he said, and stepped closer.

"No, I don't," she said, tears burning in her eyes. "What makes you think I do?"

"Because you can get it," he told her. "Real easy like."

There was something in his face that was cold. Hard. It sent chills through Leah's stomach. She wet her lips. "I'm no thief," Leah said, standing straight. She wondered if this was some terrible joke.

"Too bad," Jim said, and then shrugged. "I'm leaving day after tomorrow. You find me the money and bring it back to me, I'll consider giving you a ring."

He turned and kissed her then. It was in a rough way that Leah didn't like and made her feel cheap. Without another word, he left, leaving Leah to watch him go, her eyes wide and her heart aching.

What was she to do? A hundred and twenty dollars. That was more than she had. Jim turned the corner, and with him went her heart.

She'd wanted a ring, but not like this.

Chapter 2

Tossing the coil of rope into the back of the wagon, Stanley Keith took the opportunity to check his supplies. The wagon was filled to the brim, but he wondered if he could squeeze in a little more. A master packer, he no doubt knew he could. The problem would be if the oxen could pull the wagon with much more weight.

Considering, he looked a moment longer, then nodded. It wouldn't hurt to have a few more things. A little more medical supplies, coffee, tea, and pemmican. You couldn't have too much pemmican. The mixture of dried beef, tallow, and berries would not only sustain a man, but make for food that didn't need to be cooked, and could be eaten while walking or when he was too tired to make anything for himself.

The extra coffee and tea, well, that was essential for masking the taste of the water he might get that wouldn't be the freshest. It could be used for trade too. There would be many opportunities for trade along the way, he was sure. With other folks on the wagon train, those camped for a while, the natives, and even small settlements.

While Stanley hoped he wouldn't need to make a trade in a life-or-death situation, he sure wanted to be prepared. It would be much cheaper to buy what he needed now. The further West, the more things would cost. Especially as supplies would be scarce, and people desperate.

Extra bullets for his two guns, food enough for three, and supplies for when he started his new life in Oregon filled the wagon. The journey would be long, he knew, and tiring, but Molly had already made it with her family, and when he finally got there himself, they'd marry and stake a claim.

Molly. He hadn't seen her for almost a year. Had she changed much? He wondered if she had. She'd been a slip of a girl, sassy, full of herself, when she and her parents set out on the trail. The oldest of nine, maybe being bossy came with the territory, he wasn't sure, being the youngest of three, but somehow they'd met, fallen in love, and her parents had given their blessing for him to claim her, along with land next door, once he arrived.

An early winter had hit, and then he'd gotten hurt when he'd broken his arm, so now, starting out a little later than he'd like, made him wonder what would wait for him once he got there. He let his eye pause on a small sack where her letters rested. Filled at first with talk about their travel, her words had turned into tales of their new home.

The most recent one was very Molly-like. She told him he needed to hurry, she wasn't getting any younger and there were more men than women, so she'd find someone to replace him quickly if he wasn't there soon.

Stanley wasn't sure if that was a threat or a promise, and he also wasn't quite sure how he felt about it, but he'd made a promise to her, and aimed to fulfill it. He was a man of his word above all else. Honestly, he also looked forward to having a wife one day. He'd spent enough years alone, and knew it was time to start a family. The idea made him happy.

But of course, before he could do any of that, he had to get to Oregon. Luckily, they would be leaving soon.

He set off toward the small town to get a bite to eat. He wasn't too worried about leaving his wagon. The children in the next wagon over looked after it when he left, in exchange for a penny candy. It was well worth it for him, and he planned to stock up on the candies as well. A treat might be sorely welcome at times, and unlike some of the travelers, money wasn't much of a worry for him. He had plenty saved, and could spend as much as he needed.

Stanley whistled as he walked, feeling pretty good about leaving. Just two days and he'd be on the way. He crossed the street toward the small restaurant and paused to look at the menu posted in their window.

There was the sound of quick footsteps, and he looked up to see a young woman in a yellow dress who looked very upset coming toward him. He half wondered if he should ask if she was okay, but what could he do? He wasn't from around here, and he knew she was. With a frown, he realized he'd seen her before, working at the post office.

She passed, but a small nudge of guilt filled him. Stanley turned around to call out to her, but she was gone. Shrugging, he turned back and collided with someone.

"Beg your pardon," Stanley said. The man, a little younger than his twenty-six, just mumbled something and continued walking, his nose buried in a book.

Stanley shook his head. This place was too crowded. He looked forward to the open land and some peace. He got his meal, the supplies he was looking for, and started back to the camp and his wagon. It didn't take him long to find it, pay his fee of a lemon drop each to the Jenkins twins, and settle in.

The night came, and campfires dotted the area. A smoky smell filled his nostrils and made his nose itch. Stanley laid on the seat of his wagon and stared up at the sky. Stars were starting to come out. Navigating by them wasn't something he could do, but wondered if it was a skill he'd learn on the trail.

"Mr. Keith?"

Stanley sat up. It was the Jenkins twin's mother. She was holding her young babe tightly and looked tired. "Mrs. Jenkins," he answered.

"I wondered if you might could help me," she asked. "My husband is...my husband had to go into town for a little, and the tie on the wagon is stuck. I can't get it open to put the children in."

He sprang up. "Of course." Mrs. Jenkins didn't have to tell him where her husband was. The whole camp could smell when he returned, the drink heavy on his breath and skin. He felt sorry for her, but the woman seemed stoic in the fact. Likely, she had to be.

"Thank you," Mrs. Jenkins said, once he'd gotten the knot loose. He tipped his hat and headed back to the wagon. A movement in the town caught his eye, and for a moment, he thought he saw the woman in the yellow dress.

Before he could look closer, there was a woman's sudden scream, followed by a man's shout and yelp of pain.

Chapter 3

Leah closed her bedroom door at the boarding house and pressed her back against it. Her lips trembled, and she pressed one hand against her lips, the other against her stomach, which seemed to be hosting a field of butterflies.

What was she going to do? Something about this situation didn't feel right with Jim. Not how he treated her—he'd always treated her that way—but the money. Whenever he'd asked for it before, it wasn't much. A dollar here or there. And he'd usually bought her something small with part of it. A book, a few flowers. A bar of soap that smelled like honeysuckle.

But twenty dollars? And then to wire him a hundred more? Something just didn't feel right. No matter how she tried to ignore it, she just felt sick over his words.

Was it the tone in his voice? The cold, hardness to his eyes? The fact he'd almost threatened her? Then hinted that she might finally get a ring on her finger if she did it?

What if she didn't give him the money? He'd hinted about marriage before, but never came through with it. She wasn't sure if this time would be different, even if she did somehow give him what he wanted.

Laughter sounded through the partially open window, along with a familiar voice. Leah went to her window and stood at the side peeking through the muslin curtain. Then she gasped.

Jim was outside, seemingly unknowing where he was, with his arm around a woman she'd never seen before. And he had the nerve to ask her for money? To hint at marrying her? He was nothing but a liar! A two-timing monster!

Fury overcame Leah, and without even knowing what she was doing, she'd thrown open her door, flown down the stairs, and stomped out to the front of the boarding house.

"You no good liar!" she shouted.

Jim looked up, startled.

"You," Leah continued, poking her finger into his chest, "aren't getting another dime of my money. I never want to see you again. You're despicable, and...and..."

Leah's chest was rising and falling and she was gasping for air she was so upset at this point. The smirk on Jim's face only made her angrier.

"Jimmy, who is this?" the woman asked, confused.

By now, people had stopped in the street to watch them. Leah had a vague sense that the boarding house door was still open, the inhabitants standing and watching as well.

Jim whispered to Leah, "You'll regret this," then turned to the woman on his arm and raised his voice. "She's that crazy woman who has been all over town, offering her favors in exchange for money. She even propositioned me a few times. You know I'm not that sort of man, though."

There was a collective gasp and Leah was very aware that now, all eyes were on her. "That...that's not...you liar!" she shouted again, struck speechless at his accusation and unable to form more than the shortest of sentences.

"Come on, honey," Jim told the woman on his arm. "You don't want to be associated with a woman like that. Wouldn't even call her sort a woman, unless you put the word low or loose in front of it."

Tears burned in Leah's eyes, first of anger and injustice, then pain as Mrs. Smith, the boarding house owner, grabbed her arm. "I always wondered about you," she hissed. "Too sweet. Too polite. It was just an act, wasn't it, girl? Out you'll go. Tonight. You have five minutes to get your things."

She had to have known it would happen. You couldn't be accused of being a loose woman and expect to keep reputable lodging. Without a word, she went to her room, Mrs. Smith right behind her.

Leah pulled out her carpetbags and opened them. Mrs. Smith stood in her doorway, arms crossed. "I pay weekly," Leah said. "It's only Tuesday. I should get a refund."

"You'll get nothing but four minutes to pack," Mrs. Smith growled. "I'll not be associated with the likes of you in my place."

"I don't need your boarding house," Leah said, stuffing her dresses into her bag. "I'll find something else."

"Not in this town you won't," Mrs. Smith warned. "I doubt you still have your job."

Leah froze at that. Was...was Mrs. Smith right? She turned to look at the other woman, her voice soft. "None of what he said was true."

There was a twitch in Mrs. Smith's face. "Don't matter," she said gruffly. "Appearances are everything to folks. Especially business owners. You should have thought twice before you associated with a man like that. I could have told you he was no good, had you asked."

Lean nodded and turned. There was no time to argue. She knew Mrs. Smith would remove her before she gathered her remaining belongings if she didn't hurry. Leah finished packing and then moved to the door, a bag in each hand. Mrs. Smith followed her down the stairs. Leah stepped onto the porch and listened as the door shut behind her. It sounded so final.

She wasn't sure what to do. Where to go. She walked down the street toward the post office. Mr. and Mrs.

Gibson, the owners, lived upstairs. Perhaps just for tonight they'd take her in.

Her bags seemed as though they were filled with weights. Pride wouldn't let Leah set them down, though. She could see the post office and strode swiftly toward it. Next to it was the bank, and she hesitated when she saw the light on inside. Should she ask for her money? Goodness knows she needed it. Maybe the bank manager hadn't heard yet. Regardless, it was her money and she was owed it if she asked for it, but right now, shelter first.

Leah stood outside the post office, then took a deep breath and went around the backside, where the residence was, and knocked. Mr. Gibson opened the door. "Leah?" he asked, surprise in his voice.

Much to her dismay, Leah's lower lip trembled, and her sobs burst out before she could stop them. Mrs. Gibson rushed over and pulled her inside. "My goodness, dear. Whatever is the matter?"

Over tears and tea, Leah explained what had happened, every bit of it, to her great shame. Mr. and Mrs. Gibson were sympathetic, but shook their heads.

"You are in a terrible spot," Mrs. Gibson agreed. "I'm also afraid Mrs. Smith is right. We can't keep you on. We can't even keep you here tonight without a problem."

"What am I to do?" Leah sniffled.

Mr. Gibson frowned. "I don't know. But...wait here a moment."

He left, and Leah sat, her head hanging. "Thank you for the tea," she said quietly, just as her stomach growled.

Mrs. Gibson patted her hand. "I'll bet you had no dinner. Just a moment." She turned and cut a thick slice of freshly baked bread, and slathered it with butter. Leah gratefully ate it. It wasn't long before Mr. Gibson came back.

"I went next door to the bank. Explained what's happened. You'll want your money, I suspect. Gregory, the bank manager, you know, is stopping by in a moment. He's going to give you your money, and we are going to make a few suggestions."

"Suggestions?" Leah whispered. "Like what?"

There was a knock and Mr. Gibson opened the door. The bank manager slipped inside. He looked at Leah, then shook his head. "I expect you'll want your money before you leave town," he told her. "May I see your banking book?"

Leah nodded numbly as she looked in her handbag. "I really must leave?" she asked quietly.

"No one will hire you," Mrs. Gibson said with a shrug. "You'll also not find anyone wanting to sell you anything, not at a fair price. I'm afraid, false or not, those accusations have ruined your reputation, dear. Especially with you having met that young man in the dark several times. Someone will have seen you, and even if it was an innocent thing tongues will wag. You have no choice but to start over if you want to escape the gossip."

Sliding her banking book to the manager, Leah nodded. She understood. A terrible mistake had been made in carrying on the relationship she'd hoped would end in marriage. She saw that now. Taking a deep breath, she asked, "Well, then. That's just what I'll do." An idea formed in her mind.

The bank manager handed her over the same amount of money that was listed on her banking book. "Thank you," Leah said quietly. She stood then. "I promise not to have mentioned that any of you helped me."

Mr. and Mrs. Gibson each gave her a hug, as the bank manager left as quietly as he'd come. "I'll be praying for you, dear," Mrs. Gibson said sadly. "You were the best employee we've ever had."

"Yes," Mr. Gibson said. Then his head jerked up. "One moment. Your wages." He reached into his pocket and pulled out her wages—and a little extra.

Leah's eyes widened. "This is too much," she said.

"Go on now," Mr. Gibson said gruffly. "But be safe."

She nodded, a lump forming in her throat, and stepped through the open door. It was getting late. Soon there would be no light at all. She must seek some form of shelter.

Taking long strides down the street, Leah tried to hurry. Perhaps her plan would work. She'd had no desire to go further west than she already was, but things had taken a rather sudden turn, and her options were few.

Stopping outside of the wagon train camp, Leah looked at the scene before her. People roamed, wagons stood, and campfires burned. The air seemed to buzz with excitement. She stepped forward and asked a woman with a child, "Excuse me. Who can I talk to? I'd like to join the wagon train."

Chapter 4

Stanley jumped up and started running toward the noise. He came to a halt when he realized it was simply Mr. Jenkins, who, as he'd done before, had tried to climb into the wrong wagon after his night of drinking.

He'd just turned to head back to his own wagon when he stopped short. The woman he'd seen in town earlier in the yellow dress was there, two carpet bags at her feet, talking to the leader of the wagon train, Jeff Sanstrop.

Curious, he moved closer to hear what she was saying. He was a little too far away, but he could see the expression on her face was one of urgency, pleading, and... maybe a little desperation? A few more steps closer and he could hear.

"Please, there's got to be someone I could go with! I'll be a nanny or a cook. Tend the animals. Anything. I have no options. I simply must join."

"No unmarried women," the wagon master said firmly.

"But I—"

"No unmarried women," he said again, arms crossed. "I'll be blunt with you, miss. It's already a hard enough trip. There are going to be many times folks are going to be hungry, hurt, sick, injured. Some aren't even going to make it to the end. They'll die or settle elsewhere. We can't have an unmarried woman along. You just won't be able to do what needs to be done to take care of yourself and a wagon. Facts are facts."

"Are you married?" the woman asked. "Do you want a wife? Just for the trip? I can cook. Sort of. And—"

"Sorry, miss," the wagon master said and shook his head. "Got my wife and kids already waiting for me." He looked at her as Stanley approached. "Best of luck to you,"

Stanley stood there and watched as the wagon master left and the woman stood there looking after him. He paused, and for some reason he couldn't explain, walked up to her.

"Hello," he said. "Name's Stanley Keith. I couldn't help but overhear."

She turned and met his eyes. "Do you need a wife?"

He was taken aback at her bluntness. "I—that is—"

"I'm desperate," she told him frankly. "I'll do anything to join this wagon train to Oregon."

Mrs. Jenkins approached and wrapped an arm around the young woman. "How about we go to my wagon," she said in her quiet voice. "I've got some tea. You look like you need a friend right now. I'm not sure if I can be of any help, but I'll sure listen and try." She looked at him then, "Stanley, why don't you join us?"

He nodded, and as the woman reached for her bags, stopped her. "Let me," he said.

"Thank you," she answered. "I'm Leah. Leah Dearing."

"Well then, Leah," Mrs. Jenkins said, "I'm Claudia Jenkins. My wagon isn't too far away. Let's go."

They walked in silence for a few moments until they reached the Jenkins's wagon. Stanley set Miss Dearing's bags down and then settled himself at the campfire. There was a loud snoring coming from the back of the wagon. Sounded like Mr. Jenkins made it back to the right wagon finally.

Mrs. Jenkins pressed a mug into Leah's hands, then offered one to Stanley. "Let's enjoy this while we can," she said cheerfully. "I've been told that the further we go, the weaker our tea will be. I like mine bracing, so I was sure to pack plenty." She fixed her calm gaze on Leah. "Now then, tell us. Why are you so desperate to go to Oregon you'd marry to get there?"

***

Stanley lay looking at the stars. The camp was quiet. The night was mild, and he should have been tired. He was tired, but he couldn't sleep. Over and over in his mind, he kept seeing Miss Dearing's face.

She'd told her story, though he suspected it was a shortened version, and he was both surprised and upset by it. Clearly, the relationship the woman had been in was abusive, even if she didn't realize it. That man Jim sounded controlling.

It might start off about what she could and couldn't wear, but would quickly escalate. Leaving him was the best thing she could have done, even if it left her homeless and without a job.

At first, he wondered just why the woman would want to head out so far by herself. It wasn't like she had family there waiting for her, but when she'd explained about how she heard she could own land herself, make her own fresh start, he understood. Especially with the title of loose woman hanging over her head. A woman considered immoral or compromised wouldn't have it easy, especially without the protection of a male relative.

Stanley snorted as he shifted and tried to get comfortable. Anyone could tell just by talking to her she wasn't the sort of woman to be wearing that title. She wore an innocence on her face, even if it was mixed with determination and fire. He liked that. A woman like her could keep a man on his toes.

It was too bad there wasn't a way to help her. Facts were facts though—no unmarried women on the trail. He'd have been tempted to offer a marriage to her, just until they arrived, but for the fact Molly was waiting. He didn't want to complicate things, even if another pair of hands would be welcome at his wagon. He wasn't a complicated man, wasn't his style. Simple was how he liked things.

Sure, it would be nice not to be doing everything on his own, but he just couldn't. Molly would skin him alive.

Shifting again, his eyes roamed to the Jenkins's wagon, where Mrs. Jenkins had offered shelter to Miss Dearing until they left. He wondered what she'd do once the wagon train pulled out. Maybe he could help her find some transportation somewhere.

Or you could just marry her.

Stanley frowned. No, no, he couldn't. Molly, remember? Why was his mind telling him to do something like that?

Because she needs you.

Stanley grunted. No, she didn't. Just needed a ride out there—that was it.

So then why not marry her? Make it one of convenience. Convenient for her, convenient for you.

"And then what?" He realized he'd spoken out loud and looked around hurriedly to see if anyone had overheard him. The camp was starting to stir. Mornings came early here. Luckily, though, no one seemed to be listening.

Then you go your way to Molly, Miss Dearing goes hers, and everyone's happy. Plus you did a good deed.

"Hmm. Maybe." It honestly wasn't a bad idea. Then he'd have someone to help with the chores and the cooking. That could really be a blessing.

But still. Complicated.

Stanley stopped talking to himself. Stars were fading and morning was coming fast. Climbing off the wagon, he got the Jenkins fire stoked. He shared theirs and kept it fueled. It helped Mrs. Jenkins, but it helped him too. That was all he needed. He didn't need a temporary wife.

Mrs. Jenkins came over with fresh water and set it to boil. In a large cast iron pan, with water already in it, she scooped in several cups of dry oats, a sprinkle of salt, and set out a jug of molasses.

"We've plenty," she told Stanley. "Plan to eat with us."

"Thank you," he said, and set down a sack with a dozen apples to share.

Mr. Jenkins came and sat quietly, nursing his head, while the Jenkins children ran around, finishing morning chores and showing Miss Dearing the wagon. Stanley didn't realize he had been staring at her until Mrs. Jenkins said quietly, "Another set of hands is always welcome. She's a fine woman and I suspect a hard worker."

He looked at her. "It's a difficult trail," he said, shaking his head. "And I've got someone waiting for me. You know that."

"And she's got no one and nothing," Mrs. Jenkins said with a sigh. There was no judgment in her tone, and he knew her well enough to know she wouldn't hold blame, whatever he did. She continued, "I wish I knew a way to help her. Another man who needs a wife. Having her along would be a blessing."

Hadn't he thought something similar earlier? Stanley followed her gaze. The children, especially the baby who was rarely off of tired Mrs. Jenkins's hip, were clustered around Miss Dearing. The baby was snug in her arms, and the newcomer was laughing at something one of the twins had said.

When she laughed, her entire face lit up. It was beautiful. He caught his breath. And then he realized that despite his misgivings, and Molly, he wanted to ask Leah Dearing to marry him.

And then he'd have to keep away from her until they could get it annulled.

But there was no way he could do that. None at all. Something about her spoke to him, deep within. Stanley swallowed a lump in his throat. Marrying her and keeping his distance would be harder than the journey they were about to undertake or the pemmican in his waist pouch.

Better to ride out tomorrow on his way, and let Miss Dearing figure out her own path.

Chapter 5

"Can I talk to you a minute?" Stanley asked, approaching Leah and the Jenkins children.

"Of course," she said, and handed the baby back to its mother.

They walked a short distance away.

All around them, the people of the camp were making ready to leave tomorrow. Leah envied them. While it was true that none of them knew what the future would hold, and without a doubt the trail and the traveling would be difficult, dangerous, and even deadly for some, she still knew in her heart that Oregon was the place that she wanted to go.

There was nothing here for her. Even if she moved to another town a few miles away, her reputation would likely follow her there. Leah felt her shoulders slump as discouragement filled every inch of her. So much had changed in such a short time. She had no idea when she'd woken up the morning before that she'd be in such drastically different circumstances.

She couldn't explain the feeling deep within her, not even if someone had asked her. But Leah knew in her bones, and every inch of her could sense, that the wagon train was the best place for her to not only start over but also to build a life that she could love.

Was it perhaps the enthusiasm of others was contagious? Last night, Mrs. Jenkins had talked to her for a while about how excited she was to be going. She knew the risks, and faced them willingly, but still couldn't wait to arrive.

"I've faith," she had told Leah. "Faith in the men leading us to keep us safe, and faith in the Lord to see us there and get us settled."

She went on to talk about the wide, open spaces, the endless opportunities waiting there for them for land and building up civilization. Creating something out of very little. It set Leah's heart hammering at the idea something like that—even just a chance at such a thing—could possibly be hers.

Most of the night, Leah had thought about Oregon and wondered how she could get herself there too. It didn't seem uncommon that women had to be married to go on wagon trains. In fact, two women at a distance were pointed out by Mrs. Jenkins as wives chosen only a few days before. So, how could she also find a husband quickly?

Sleep, though she longed for the oblivion of it, hadn't come—not with all of her worry. That morning, she'd hoped things would work themselves out, but didn't feel confident they would. When Stanley had asked to speak with her, she knew there wouldn't be anything good to come of the conversation. She hoped she was wrong, but Leah was used to disappointment. This time would be no different.

Now and then, as she and Stanley walked through the camp in silence, she stole glances at him under her lashes. What was it he wanted? Had he perhaps changed his mind about marrying her? Her breath caught at the idea, and she hoped desperately it was so. However, the frown on his face was saying otherwise, and it wasn't looking good for her.

Surely if there'd been another man in need of a wife, Mrs. Jenkins would have pointed him out?

He still hadn't spoken, so, timidly, she asked, "Have you...changed your mind about marrying me?" She quickly added, her words tumbling out in a rush, "Mrs. Jenkins told me you had a woman waiting for you. That you...that you couldn't. But..." she didn't say anything else. Leah was unsure what to say. Not without risking the tears that weren't far from the surface.

Stanley stopped and opened his mouth, just as a man pushing fifty at least, with more wrinkles than face, and a smell that showed he didn't know what a bar of soap looked like, came up to her.

"Hear ya need a husband," he said with a grin, displaying several missing teeth, the rest stained brown. "I'll marry ya," he added. "Ya sure are pretty. Look fine on my arm." He held out his arm and pretended to walk with her alongside of him.

Leah stiffened. When she had thought about a marriage of convenience, this aspect, one of an undesirable pairing, wasn't what she'd thought about. She hadn't realized this could be one of the options for her husband. An involuntary shiver ran over her, and a warm arm reached around her. She startled at the touch, but leaned into it, instinctively.

"Sorry, Harry. A bit too late," Stanley said. "I'm afraid that Miss Dearing and I are getting married."

She looked at him, hoping she was doing a good job of masking the surprise on her face.

"Aww shucks," Harry answered. He spat loudly on the ground, and Leah shuddered again. He looked up at them and groaned while slapping at one knee. "If only I hadnta stopped for my morning chaw. Ya beat me out. Can't keep up with young folk no more. Too fast for the likes of me." He turned and shuffled away.

Leah waited until he was out of earshot, then turned to Stanley. "Do you mean that?" She was trying to keep her voice calm. Not show her hope and excitement. After all, he might have just been saying they were marrying to save her from an unwanted situation. Another shiver came over her. What if he'd lied just to protect her? How many other men like Harry might be willing to marry her? And was that the only way that she'd make it out West? Marrying a man like him? A surge of despair filled her.

Stanley removed his arm from around her shoulder and shoved his hands in his pockets. "Yeah. I guess so. Just until we're there. Then, we'll annul it. We have to. Molly's waiting for me."

Leah's temper flared, and she put her hands on her hips. She opened her mouth to say something, then closed it again. She'd take a guess so and an annulment over an offer from Harry any day. Besides, he already had someone he was promised to. Molly. Whoever she was. It wouldn't be fair to that other woman, and she likely wouldn't be happy knowing that her intended was marrying someone else—even just to rescue her, a stranger. Gratitude was what was needed here, not irritation.

Nodding, she said quietly, "Thank you. What do I need to do to get ready? I have all of my belongings in those two bags, but I doubt that's enough for the trail."

He got a thoughtful look and rubbed at his jaw as he spoke. "I've the supplies already, and food enough for us both. I don't know what womanly things you might need? More clothing? You'll want another pair or two of shoes, that I am sure of."

"I have two in my carpetbag," Leah assured. "I'll just ask Mrs. Jenkins. If there's anything more I need, I could get it in town." Then she stopped. "No, I doubt they'd sell it to me." Her shoulders slumped.

"If there's something you need, give me a list," he said. "We won't go without it, as long as they have it in the store."

Leah couldn't stop the gratitude that was in her voice. "Thank you," she said. She reached out and took his hand between hers. His was so large, it peeked out between hers, but she still squeezed gently. "I appreciate this," she said. "I will do the best job that I can to help you."

He nodded, and shuffled his feet, looking a little uncomfortable. "Well, I'll go find the preacher," Stanley told her. "See when we can be wed. He's around here somewhere."

He walked off, leaving her to wonder if the last few moments had really happened. Was she really going to be getting married? And heading to Oregon?

Excitement filled her, and she hurried back to Mrs. Jenkins. The other woman would surely know if she needed anything more.

When she walked up, Mrs. Jenkins smiled at her. "Breakfast is ready. Have a bowl."

Leah took the offered tin bowl and spoon and sat next to Mrs. Jenkins. She whispered, "Stanley asked me to marry him."

The other woman's smile mirrored her own and her eyes grew wide. "Really? That's wonderful," she said.

"It's just until we get there," Leah said, letting out a small sigh. Then she straightened her shoulders. "That's fine with me, though. As long as I get there to this place of opportunities, I don't care how I arrive."

Mrs. Jenkins reached over and squeezed her hand. "I know he had someone waiting for him, but that doesn't mean she still is. Perhaps you'll have more than a marriage of a few months."

"It doesn't bother me at all," Leah said. She smiled broadly, "I'm going, and that's all that matters to me!"

"This is such good news," Mrs. Jenkins said. "And we'll be traveling together!" The other woman looked excited as she clasped her hands together.

"I'll help you however I can," Leah promised. Then she asked, "What do I need personally to bring that he might not have already?"

Mrs. Jenkins thought a moment. "You'll want an extra bonnet. One with a large brim. Sewing supplies. Some tea. He's a coffee drinker. A blank book and pencils so you can write."

Leah nodded and made a list on a scrap of paper she had in her bag. When Stanley returned a short time later, over bites of oatmeal, he told her that the pastor would marry them that evening. Then, taking her list, he made his way to town to get what she requested. Meanwhile, Leah helped Mrs. Jenkins wash the dishes.

"Thank you for helping me," Mrs. Jenkins said. "And please, remember to call me Claudia."

"It's the least I can do," Leah said. "You took me in and I will be grateful forever. I'm glad we are friends, Claudia. It will be nice traveling with you. Perhaps we will settle near each other."

"Yes, it will be wonderful," Claudia agreed. "Though, I am sorry about your circumstances."

Leah sighed. "There's nothing I can do about it. But when we get there, I'll start over."

"What do you think you'll do?" Claudia asked. "What skills have you to support yourself?"

"I don't know. I've always worked in a store or the post office. But everyone talks about how the West is so full of opportunity. If I don't find it, then I'm sure it will find me," Leah said, more confidently than she felt.

But the rest of the day, up until the moment that Stanley and she said "I do" before the assembled members of the wagon train, Claudia's question kept bothering her. She would be on her way in the morning, and what then? There was one comfort, at least. She had several months to figure it out.

Her excitement of starting fresh had already waned, as she realized that once she arrived in Oregon, she'd be alone. Staking a claim, building a house, planning a future...it all suddenly seemed too much for one person.

Chapter 6

From his seat on the wagon, Stanley glanced down at Leah. It was their fourth day traveling with the wagon train. He'd taught her how to drive the team, but to keep the burden as light as possible on the oxen, they took turns walking.

She was there next to Mrs. Jenkins, and the two were collecting whatever firewood they could as they walked, gathering it into their aprons until they had bundles large enough to toss into the back of the wagon.

The further they got along the trail, the less they'd find. The guide had warned them to collect as much as they could while they could, and to seek out things such as pine cones and even dried dung in order to help fuel the nighttime fires.

At first, some of the women and men had looked horrified at the suggestion, but when it was explained that later it would be the only fuel available to cook their meals, they nodded. It also helped to know that the dung chips would also burn without producing a smell, and burn hot because of all the grass inside of them.

Stanley would be the first to admit that he was surprised at the size of the buffalo chips, for the majority of the dung they came across was from those beasts. The dried excrement was flattened, almost the size of a dinner plate. They'd been warned that it might be wise to keep a small store of fuel in a dry place, for if it rained, the chips would take on moisture and not burn. He wondered what kind of weather they'd have as they pressed forward. Would there be much rain?

So far the weather had been mild, and their party had fared well. As that wasn't always the case, and they were still early in the trip, he hoped their luck held.

"Stanley?"

He glanced over at Leah, who was looking at him, a little tiredly. "Do you want to drive for a while?" he offered.

She bit her lip, then shook her head. "No, I can walk just a little longer. I admit, my legs and my feet ache, and I'm pretty sure my blisters have blisters growing on them. I'm not used to this much walking. What I wondered was, how far do you think we've come so far?"

"Today? About twelve miles," he told her. "Just another six to go if we can,"

The wagon trail tried to do eighteen miles each day. Occasionally they'd do more if possible, but there would be days they had to do far less, such as if the weather was poor, so each mile behind them was valuable. Eighteen was the goal, especially while they were so early in their journey, and not as tired or weak yet. Before setting out, it was warned that anyone too weak to continue would be left behind the next morning. There was no turning back for any reason at all.

She was quiet a moment. "Maybe I would like to drive, if I can," she said. "For a little, if you don't mind?"

He nodded, stopped the oxen, and jumped down. Mrs. Jenkins was also switching with her husband. Stanley offered his hand to Leah, and shyly she took it and his help in climbing into the wagon seat.

"Thank you," she said softly, giving him a tired smile.

As she settled on the seat and started the team, he couldn't help but admire her. Leah was a little different from how he'd originally thought she might be. He didn't really think she'd do well on the trail, but she'd surprised him each day. She woke before dawn, helped prepare breakfast, and readied the wagon for travel. At nooning, when they stopped an hour for a meal and to rest both the beasts and the humans, she prepared lunch, fetched water, and sometimes washed a piece or two of laundry or did some other chore.

As she walked, she was always hunting for fuel for the fire or making sure if they passed clean water that their barrel of drinking water was filled. Though the dust swirled everywhere from the animal hooves and the sun beat down hotter than anything he'd felt before, she didn't complain once.

Sure, not every day would be like that, this trip would take its toll and there would be days of exhaustion where a grumble might be the only thing to get them through, but he still had the feeling that she'd make it to the end of their journey, and with that determined expression on her face. Or one of her beautiful smiles.

Leah's face was expressive and could switch in a moment. He'd seen storm clouds in her eyes that vanished in a blink as happiness overcame her face. She was a constant surprise in how she spoke or acted, and he found it delightful. She wasn't spoiled in the least, but always worked hard, pitching in even without being asked. He could grow to love a woman like that.

The thought jolted him, and he frowned, looking away from her quickly. He had to remember Molly. After all, she'd been waiting for him. This was a marriage of convenience only. And so far, that's just how they'd kept it.

At night, Leah slept in the wagon alone. He slept on the bench of the wagon or on a bedroll on the ground. So far, no one had said anything about it, figuring that he was doing his part to help keep an eye out for any dangers that might attack the wagon party. Other men were doing the same, and watches had been established.

When it was dark and everyone was sleeping was the perfect time for a wild animal or someone unsavory with trouble on their mind to attack and hurt them. It couldn't even be ruled out that it would be someone from their own party, which is why the watches rotated, as did the men who were placed on them.

Thankfully, they'd not run into anything like that just yet, but he was sure it would only be a matter of time. Humans were that way. If someone were to get desperate, they might do something foolish. The same could be said for a wild animal. That's why watches were so important, for both the humans and their supplies, but also their beasts. After all, they had not only animals of their own, but food that could likely be smelled at a distance by those with sharp senses.

A creek rose ahead and Stanley jogged to the front of the team. Every time, he'd had to urge them across the water crossings. The days were warm enough that his clothes dried fairly quickly, but he worried what would happen as the weather grew cooler if they hadn't made it to Oregon before the snow. Crossing a creek or river and getting chilled could kill a man.

As the wagons crossed the moving water, he was grateful this one wasn't up past his knees and it also wasn't wider than about ten feet. The oxen could handle that easily. Yesterday, they'd crossed a river, and even at the shallow crossing, where it had been marked as safe for the wagon train, it had come near to his head. He'd swam across, tugging on the oxen who didn't care for the water, to get them loaded onto the raft for the crossing.

It was more dangerous than some would imagine. If an animal got upset or scared, it could hurt you. If a wagon couldn't float or tipped, people might be injured and the precious supplies could and would be ruined. The further they went, the more devastating the loss of foodstuffs would be, or the tools to repair wagons.

It was only a matter of time before the wagon wheels or an axle or some other part, like one of the oxen's yokes, would need a repair. Without the tools, he'd be stuck at the mercy of whoever could help—and at whatever cost.

After they came to the opposite bank of the creek, Stanley squeezed water from his pants legs, trying to dry himself. The sun was starting to lower, and it wasn't quite hot enough to dry him quickly. Walking in wet pants wasn't comfortable, but there was no use in complaining. What would it do?

"Do you want a warm drink? The kettle is still hot," Leah said.

"Might like that," he agreed, and reached for the mug she handed him.

After nooning, she'd kept the kettle filled, and they each enjoyed drinking the wildflower tea she'd made. It was a welcome treat and helped save their tea and coffee. Leah and Mrs. Jenkins had picked, and were drying in the back of the wagons, dandelions, wild peppermint, and some thistles. It was their hope to be able to stretch their current supplies by foraging.

As he accepted the tin mug, their fingers brushed, and he found himself wishing, not for the first time, that this wasn't just a marriage of convenience.

All around the camp, he'd been congratulated on his beautiful wife. What would they say if they knew that it was in name only? While he knew for a fact it wasn't uncommon to have such a thing, the part that others would find odd was that Leah was a woman who worked hard, cooked well, and was easy on the eyes. Not only that, she smiled often and sang, her voice sweet and clear. That made the walking a little easier.

He could just imagine the questions, the stares, the headshakes, when people found out that not only had they not consummated their marriage, that they'd be getting it annulled. They'd wonder what was wrong with him. Of course, he sure didn't plan to go telling anything to anybody. It wasn't even so much about his pride as it was also the need for protection for Leah. She had a mantle of security around her being a married woman. One that might not exist if anyone knew the marriage wasn't real.

Claudia Jenkins knew, he was sure. The woman was sharp, observed everything, but she and Leah had become fast friends, close friends, and he was sure that the slightly older woman would never betray Leah. It made him happy that they had connected so well. Mrs. Jenkins needed that, and he could tell Leah did too.

"What was that?"

Leah's concern broke him from his thoughts, and he saw her pointing. Whatever it was she'd seen, others were now seeing too. From his viewpoint on the ground, Stanley couldn't see what she was motioning to. A sea of white canvas covers stretched overtop towering wagons blocked whatever it was that was causing alarm, and the wagons to slow.

He swung up onto the slowing wagon and raised a hand to shield his eyes from the afternoon sun. After a brief moment, he saw where she had gestured. He reached beneath the wagon seat and pulled out his rifle, setting it by his feet.

"Pack of coyotes," he said grimly. "It's a surprise to see them out right now. We'll keep watch on them. They shouldn't bother us during the day. They must be feeling desperate to do something so risky."

"But at night?"

He didn't miss the worry in her tone. "At night, whoever is on guard will be watching to protect the people and the livestock. No man on this wagon train is unarmed, and many of the women know how to shoot."

Leah was quiet as he sat next to her. He wouldn't stay next to her for long, but it was obvious this had her worried, and he didn't want to leave her until she'd calmed down and the coyotes were well out of sight. That fact, combined with the scent of roses coming from her hair, made him want to stay as long as he could.

"You okay?" he asked quietly. He hoped she knew he was concerned about her. Would protect her. Because he would.

She nodded as she turned her head toward him. "Yes," she answered, with a small sigh that was little more than a puff of air exhaling. "Just...just I hope that we make it there safely. I didn't realize how dangerous it would be to make this trip. Not really. I knew hardships would be aplenty. Things like hard work and being tired. Bad weather and no real roof over one's head. That was to be expected, but the danger. I...I was woefully unaware of all that could go wrong."

"Because of the animals?" he asked.

"Not just them." She was quiet a moment, and her fingers tightened around the reins. She took in a shaky breath, then said, her voice a near whisper, "I heard that some of us won't make it there. Accidents and injuries from the river crossings, starvation, wagon or animal accidents, illnesses...the list goes on. I overheard some of the women talking about it." She turned her troubled eyes to him, and before he realized what he was doing, Stanley rested his hand on top of hers.

"Leah, I promise you, you'll make it there," he said, his voice low. "I'm not going to let anything happen to you."

Her eyes searched his, and she almost had a pleading expression on her face. She looked so vulnerable, so small, it awakened a fierce desire to protect her not just on this journey, but for the rest of his life, however long it was. A strand of her hair had worked its way loose, and Stanley reached over and pushed it out of her eyes. His thumb lingered, tracing over her cheek.

He wanted nothing more than to lean in and kiss her. To give her comfort, make sure she knew that he'd do all he could to take care of her, and he meant it. He'd started to move toward her, his eyes on her lips, when that face, the one he knew was waiting for him, came to mind.

Molly.

Chapter 7

Stifling a yawn, Leah rubbed the sleep from her eyes and stumbled from the back of the wagon. All around her, other women were doing the same.

Morning came early. Far earlier than back home—well, her old life. She hadn't been home for a long time, and she didn't really have a home at the boarding house. Since her mother remarried a few years prior and her stepfather favored his own daughters, not her, she decided to make her own way.

Up until the problems with Jim, she'd been doing just fine. At least, she thought she had been. Now Leah had a sinking suspicion that maybe she hadn't. Seeing how much Claudia and some of the other women cared for their daughters made her realize how betrayed she felt by her family.

If her mother had taken better care of her, told her new husband that they needed to help Leah, find her a good man in time and let her live at home until that day, would she have maybe been living a different life now? Perhaps happily married? Or maybe helping her mother around her house, working somewhere during the day at a job she liked?

She had rather liked the post office. Jim had taken that away. Just like, she realized now, he'd tried to take away so many other things. When she thought back, she'd never had a close friend. It was always and only Jim from almost the moment she'd moved into the town. He'd kept her away from everyone else, promising to look after her. Protect her.

But she'd be darned if she didn't wear that yellow dress with pride now. She might always wear yellow. She wasn't going to let his dislikes stop her.

In the end, would not wearing the dresses he didn't like have made a difference? She didn't think so. When he didn't get what he wanted, he betrayed her. Who knows if he'd done it before. Jim was only using her for what he could get, and when she finally said no, he left her in a most life changing way. He took away her room, her job, the town she was used to. He'd taken away everything.

Leah blinked back tears as she grew closer to the campfire, the bucket of water in hand. No, she wouldn't think like that. He might have ruined those things for her, but she now had something more. Something better.

Claudia, her first true friend in so long, and the chance at a new life. And...Stanley. If she could claim Stanley? Leah let out a sigh. He was complicated in the way he acted. She didn't like that. She understood it, though. He'd been put into a tough spot, however, he'd protected her. Kept her safe. Showed concern.

All of those things confused her. Was he simply being nice? Or was he starting to feel something for her, the way she was feeling for him? Of course, it was a fact that being around someone all the time could lead to feelings growing, of one kind or another. She was grateful they were the kind of affection, not of disgust, like that other man who'd offered to marry her would have given her.

But there might be other feelings in her, and when she thought about it, one sprang to mind. Love. Sometimes she felt there was a little hint of that in her heart.

And just as quickly pushed it aside.

Stanley had a woman waiting on him. He'd made that clear from the start and she needed to respect that, respect him, and respect his intended. It made her curious, though. What kind of woman must Molly be, that Stanley was willing to travel so far to be with her? To wait for so long for her?

Molly must be very special. And each time Leah thought about that, she couldn't help but feel a little jealous. She wanted to be special. To have someone care about her, the way Stanley cared about Molly.

"Thank you, Leah," Claudia said, jarring her out of her thoughts as the other woman took the bucket. "I can't believe I knocked over the other one."

"It's so early," Leah said with a yawn. "It's hard for me not to stumble some days. I consider it a wonder that it wasn't me who kicked it. I'm all thumbs and clumsy until we actually get started walking. You'd think I'd be used to it by now."

Claudia laughed and nodded. "Yes. When we get to Oregon, you won't find me waking up a bit earlier than I need to!"

Leah joined in the laughter and started stirring the cornmeal mush. Stanley had looked up at their shared giggles from where he was hitching the oxen and grinned at her. She smiled back, her heart growing a little lighter at his attention, even if her eyes felt heavy.

The early rising was a necessity, though. It took time to pack up and get moving, and while the men worked on preparing them for the trail ahead, some even riding in front as scouts on their horses, the women made breakfast.

Breakfasts were oats or porridge usually, and often bacon. Bread dough was made, so that it could rise during the day and be baked later. Depending on the rest of the menu, beans were put on to soak, or more water was added from when they started soaking the night before. At night, usually beans and bacon or a thick stew was the evening meal.

Leftovers were eaten for the midday meal, as there wasn't much time to cook, so Leah had taken to making several batches of bread dough each morning, so that they'd have plenty of bread at each meal, or if needed as a snack while walking, along with some of the jerky or dried apples. Claudia often made johnnycakes, and both wagons would share whatever extra they had.

It was hard work cooking on the trail, and Leah was incredibly grateful that Claudia was very skilled at it. They shared fires and often cooked their food together. Sometimes Leah and Stanley would give the supplies and Claudia would cook the main meal, while Leah would make the bread or gather extra water.

Many hands make for light work, she'd often heard, and it was true. After three weeks on the trail, she was growing more used to the walking, and her legs were stronger. That didn't stop her from feeling tired, though. She'd lost a few pounds too, she was sure, from all of the walking.

Others were tired as well. It was to be expected, however, they still had so much more distance to travel and a long time to journey together. Squabbles broke out in the camp here and there, and often over the smallest of things. You never knew what it would be. Sometimes the person upset didn't even make sense as to why they were upset.

Leah and Stanley and the Jenkins stayed out of the disputes. The travel was hard enough, they didn't need someone upset at them because they sided one way or another.

The weather had continued to hold, at least. It hadn't rained at all yet, something that at first she considered lucky. If it did rain, the trail would become muddy and it would be difficult to get through. However, that made getting fresh water difficult sometimes. So far, they'd not had a problem, but would their luck continue to hold? She hoped it would.

"Breakfast is ready," Claudia called.

Everyone gathered around, the twins sitting near Leah. She smiled at them, and then smiled bigger as Stanley slipped each of the children a peppermint stick, and put a finger to his lips.

The children giggled and thanked him, while Claudia gave him a grateful look. Mr. Jenkins had wandered over to a neighbor, and they were having a liquid breakfast. Leah couldn't help but feel bad for her friend. Claudia never complained, but it was obvious her having to take care of almost everything on her own weighed her down at times. It made her glad to help however she could, and she suspected that's why Stanley had brought that little stash of candy along, for the children.

Mr. Jenkins had been in the Army, Claudia had told Leah one day. He'd seen some terrible things, had to do some terrible things he'd told her. Drinking was how he coped, how he forgot for a time. She didn't fault him, though she wished there was a better way for him to manage his upset.

The times he was sober, he was cheerful, playing with his children and making the most incredible music on a fiddle. Leah could see why Claudia had fallen for him many years before.

"We might get rain today," Stanley said, looking up at the sky. He startled her from her thoughts. When had he drawn so near to her?

"Do you think so?" Leah asked, scooping up the breakfast and handing him a bowl and spoon.

"Thank you. I do," Stanley said. "Not because we seem due for it, but the signs."

"What signs?" Leah asked. She really had no idea how he could tell.

He motioned to the sky with his spoon, and everyone's eyes followed. "Those clouds. See how puffy they are?"

The sun was only just starting to wake, but Leah could see.

"It's also a little cooler than usual, and the wind has picked up. Sometimes the gusts come from one direction, and then another. Those are all signs."

The wagon master shouted loudly, and everyone quieted and drew closer to him. "We're leaving early," he called. "There's rain coming, and we should get as far as we can. We go in ten minutes."

Everyone quickly ate, and Leah gathered the dishes, dropping them into the bucket of water. "I'll wash them," she told Claudia. "Can you get the supplies packed?"

"Yes. Children," Claudia said. "Help me, quickly."

"Best look for some fuel for the fire as we go," Stanley said. "That way we can at least make a small fire to cook if it's drizzling."

"Yes. I don't have much," Leah said. "It has been so mild. With no rain at all, I admit, I let the emergency fuel dwindle, so that it was less weight for the oxen."

"Everyone did," Stanley said. "Which may make it harder to collect some."

There was a shout and the wagons started to pull out. "I'll start hunting now," Leah promised, and pulled out a large basket she hooked on her arm.

"I'll take over in an hour," he promised, and climbed into the wagon seat.

The morning passed quietly, with no sight of rain. Still, Leah collected buffalo chips and bundles of dry grass, and filled her basket. When Stanley switched with her for the second time, she enjoyed the view from the wagon and the chance to rest her feet.

Right now, they were going through a valley. Time and travelers had caved a path through tall rock formations. She marveled at the way they stacked atop each other.

Sometimes, she could see the different color layers in the rocks, and it fascinated her. Oranges and yellows and browns of all shades blended into an image she hoped she'd never forget. Leah wished she had the talent to paint. She'd have loved to capture the formations. Tonight, she'd have to write in her journal about all she saw. She didn't want to ever forget the majestic sights she'd witnessed on this journey.

There had been everything from enormous birds flying overhead to fields of spring flowers, and a massive herd of buffalo that slowly lumbered through the plains. Some came so close to the wagons she could hardly believe it. There had been so much to see, and now, these impressive formations. At times, she wondered over the beauty, how it was almost unimaginable. She was grateful to have a chance to see it for herself.

Stanley was walking alongside the wagon, talking to another man. Leah watched them for a moment, then looked away. She didn't want it to seem like she was eavesdropping. News was one thing Leah missed. Information and stories that were new. They had no way to receive any of that here.

The sky grew dark then, almost at once, and she looked up with a frown, then toward Stanley who was doing the same. They glanced at each other, then toward the man on horseback leading the group. His arm was waving, meaning to press forward. They wouldn't stop unless they had to. Each mile was too precious. The rider moved faster, and a shout from the lead wagon showed they were trying to increase their pace as well.

A fat raindrop hit Leah, then another. Soon, it was pelting on her. The wind picked up, and the icy drops stung her exposed skin. "Won't we stop?" she gasped, leaning toward Stanley.

"No," he answered, urgency in his voice. "Press them faster." The other wagons had sped up, and Stanley leaped up into the wagon, urging the oxen to go faster.

Leah scanned his face. It was tense. The rain was heavy now. She could get into the back of the wagon, but a surge of fear ran through her. "You aren't telling me something," she said, her voice low and tight. "What's wrong?"

There was indecision in his eyes. The oxen, though they were pulling hard, were starting to slip as mud formed.

"We are in a valley," Stanley finally said, his mouth close to her ear. It was the only way to hear him over the now pounding rain and howling wind. "If we don't get out, and the storm washes the rain down through the valley…"

He didn't finish. He didn't have to. Leah's whole body tightened with fear. The wagons were single file, the Jenkins family behind them.

The rain beat faster, and Leah closed her eyes. Would they make it through?

Chapter 8

The rain began to pour even harder—if that was possible. Torrential downpour was the only way Leah could describe it. End of the world, flood-making, perhaps. Leah peered through the small flap in the wagon's back. Stanley had ordered her inside, where she could dry off and have some protection from the rain.

Claudia and her children were also inside of their wagon, with Mr. Jenkins at the reins, a tense expression on his face. To see him looking as concerned as he did made Leah feel more alarmed than she had at Stanley's frightening words.

"If we don't get out, and the storm washes the rain down through the valley..."

She gulped down the lump of fear rising from her stomach to her throat. Leah closed her eyes and prayed.

They were close. Another mile. But the oxen had slowed as the mud grew thicker. The rain was so fast, it was starting to collect, and the hooves of the animals made a splashing sound. They were hardly creeping forward now, and the slow speed made the oxen's heavy feet stick in the mud. A sickening slurping sound was made each time a hoof raised, and at times an ox would stumble and the wagon shudder.

They couldn't go any faster. But if they didn't...No. She refused to think about that. Refused to let her imagination grow wild. Still, a shiver came over her as she imagined the settlers getting hit by the force of the water, and the wagons unable to fight against it. What would happen? Who would survive?

Outside, she could hear Stanley shouting at the oxen. The sound of his voice sent chills through her. Mr. Jenkins was doing the same to his team.

"Almost there!" Stanley yelled.

Leah closed her eyes in relief. She was shivering almost uncontrollably. Unsure if it was from the chill of the damp in the air or her fear, she didn't know and didn't care. She wrapped a blanket around herself and anxiously waited for the wagon to stop.

After what seemed like an hour, but was likely much less, the wagon slowed, then stopped. Stanley pushed his way in, soaked and shivering. Leah gasped when she saw him and quickly grabbed blankets.

"Got to get my clothes off," Stanley said, teeth chattering. "I'm sorry."

"Don't be," Leah said briskly. She reached for some of his dry clothing. "You'll get sick if you don't." She handed him the clothing and turned her back.

There was a sloshing sound and a few drops hit her as he peeled off his clothes and dropped them to the wagon's floor near her feet. A moment later she turned, holding two thick blankets in her arms. "Wrap these around you," she said. "I wish we had something hot to drink."

Leah peered through the wagon. The Jenkins's wagon was parked nearby. Inside, Mr. Jenkins must be doing the same as Stanley. She closed her eyes a moment and let out a sigh of relief. It felt so good to be stopped. She was grateful they'd made it through, and Claudia and her family as well. Hopefully, everyone did.

"You okay?" Stanley asked, his teeth chattering.

"I'm fine," she answered, and then wrapped their other two blankets around him.

He closed his eyes for a moment. "That was...scary," he admitted, as he opened his eyes. "I'm glad we made it through."

"Me too," Leah said. She bit her lip. "Thank you for getting us through safely."

"I promised to protect you," Stanley told her, his eyes burning into her. He reached a hand out and found hers.

She sucked in her breath. The only light was from the small lantern she had hanging, and the sudden intimacy of the moment made Leah blush. She was glad it was unlikely he could tell.

"You're so warm," Stanley said, letting out a deep sigh. It was then she noticed how cold his skin was.

Leah moved closer. "Here. Let me sit next to you. You'll warm up quicker."

Stanley opened the cocoon of blankets and pulled her close. The chill of his body removed any sort of worry or awkwardness. Leah snuggled into him and soon felt him warm. His shivering stopped, as did hers. A sense of peace came over her, and her eyelids drooped.

***

She wasn't sure how long had passed, but Leah woke to Stanley's arms around her. He felt so strong and comforting. So warm and delicious. It was as though his arms were made simply to be around her. Still half asleep, she nuzzled closer, then realized what she was doing.

What about Molly?

The unknown woman came between them, again, and she bit her lip. It didn't matter that she might want to have more with Stanley than a marriage of convenience. That woman was there, and in the way. It was hard not to think about her, and when Leah thought for too long about her, it was torture.

Somehow, along the journey, Stanley had become...hers. The thought made her shake her head, press her lips together. That was silly. He wasn't hers. Not really. And she'd known that all along. Leah studied Stanley for a moment. He was so brave, so strong. It had taken a lot of effort to get the oxen through the valley. He'd stayed outwardly calm. She knew she wouldn't have been able to do that.

That wasn't all he'd done over the last several weeks. He'd cared for her, treated her with respect, made her feel appreciated, and wanted, and welcome. Those were all things she'd never really felt at all in her life. Leah's fingers longed to run themselves over his face.

He was beautiful when he slept, she realized. Long, dark lashes that hid his thoughtful eyes, a softening of his face that was tanned from the sun, even though he wore a hat. A hint of whiskers were on his face and—

Her thoughts broke off as Stanley stirred, then opened his eyes. "Something wrong?" he asked, sitting up quickly.

"No, not at all," Leah said, easing back.

"Are you sure?" He frowned, and looked around, then leaned over and peered through the wagon cover's crack. "You looked like you were about to say something."

Leah shrugged, and flushed slightly. "No, I was just thinking," she said quietly.

"About what?" He fixed her with that piercing stare he was so good at. The one that tried to read inside of her soul, to puzzle her out.

After thinking for a moment, Leah figured there was no harm in telling him. "I was thinking how brave you were yesterday. How I'd have never been able to get the oxen across without being scared. You saved our lives."

The reality of what she said sank in, and her voice caught at the final words. Stanley grabbed her hands and squeezed them gently. Leah looked at his large hands covering hers, and tears sprang to her eyes. Soon, those hands would cover Molly's fingers, wouldn't they? She couldn't even enjoy this moment of being close to him without thinking about her.

"Look at me," Stanley said softly. When she raised her head, he continued, "You could have done it. You'd have been brave enough. You are brave enough. I've never met a woman with more gumption than you. Nothing stops you. You do what needs doing, even if it's hard or dirty or scary."

Leah didn't answer, just listened. His words eased an ache within her. Like a thirsty soul, she drank them in.

He continued, "I'll tell you the truth. I was scared. Terrified. I knew the water was rising. A flash flood was inevitable. I was worried I'd not be able to get us through, and if I couldn't go faster that even if we made it, the wagons behind us might not."

At her shudder, he nodded. "You knew it too, didn't you?"

"We all did," Leah said, taking a deep breath. "It was a dangerous position to be in."

He nodded and sat back a little, still holding one of her hands. His thumb rubbed over her knuckles, and Leah wondered if he realized it. She watched his thumb as it made a slow stroke one way, then back again. It was almost mesmerizing.

"I hope we don't have to do anything like that again, but I'm worried about the next few days," he admitted.

"Why?" she asked. "The rain has stopped. Though the road is muddy, we should hopefully be able to travel soon."

But what he said next chilled her more than the rain and wind had last night.

"It's not the mud. It's the river we must cross next. Swollen and overflowing from the storm, and deadly."

Chapter 9

Stanley sopped up the peppered flour gravy with his chunk of bread, then ate it. As he chewed, he glanced around the wagon train. It had been two days since their trip through the valley when it had rained so heavily. Not an hour went by without him thinking how grateful he was they'd made it out alive.

That was nothing, though, compared to what they'd face today.

For a day, the wagon train had camped out, allowing the roads to get less muddy and the river they needed to cross to hopefully calm. Now, it was nearing the moment of truth. The ground was still soggy, but the wagons could move. Slowly, but progress was progress, and now he knew how those deep ruts that made their wagon jolt and bounce were made. Wet ground and heavy wagons.

If all went well, they'd cross the river around midday. He hoped the waters would be calm. The wagons could float, and ropes would be used to help guide it on a raft made for the wagons, but if the waters were too rough, they'd be delayed longer. If they were only a little turbulent, it would be up to the wagon master's discretion.

"Time to go!" a voice shouted, and Stanley quickly stood. Leah took his bowl and washed it, then tossed the water from the bucket to the ground.

She assumed her usual position, walking near the wagon, basket in one hand and an eye out for fuel for the fire. As she walked along, Stanley couldn't help but stare at her. Since that night they'd huddled together for warmth, he'd not been able to get her out of his mind. She'd fit perfectly next to him.

The sweetness of her face as she'd rested against his chest pleased him. His breath caught every time he thought about it. He could have stared at her for hours. Truth be told, when he was driving that wagon, he was scared. Terrified. The only thing he could think about was getting Leah to safety. When they'd finally made it out of the valley, he'd near collapsed with relief to see her alive and well.

That night, her tucked against him, awoke a fierce range of emotions in him. He'd already had that, but now...it was much greater. The sensation struck him as odd. He'd never felt that way about Molly. Granted, he'd never spent the night with Molly, that wasn't proper, but even riding together in the wagon when they'd had an opportunity to hold hands or sit close, he'd never felt the same things with Molly that he felt with Leah.

Comfortable. Protective. Proud.

It confused him, and he had been thinking nonstop about it. He liked taking care of Leah. It upset him each time he thought about how she'd been taken advantage of, and practically run out of the town. How could anyone who knew her think that she'd be a loose woman? A flash of anger surged through him, and he hoped for half a moment he did run across Jim one day. He'd teach that man a lesson he'd not soon forget. His actions were no way to treat a lady.

As if she sensed him thinking about her, Leah looked up. Stanley smiled at her. When she returned his smile, his stomach did a strange flipping thing. He'd never get used to that, how just a single look from her could do that.

Would she still look at him that way years from now? He hoped so. But just as soon as he had that thought, he remembered. It was impossible for that to happen. He and Leah were parting ways soon.

Night before last, he'd laid on the wagon seat trying to sleep and wondering if he could figure a way out of this mess. He'd not intended on being interested in Leah, in falling in love. But that's what he was doing. He knew it wasn't fair to Molly, making her think he loved her when maybe he didn't. It also wasn't fair to Leah, and he hoped he wasn't leading her on somehow. Surely, though, she understood that their days were limited and wasn't having near the problem that he was.

She'd just felt so right in his arms though. And Stanley just couldn't stop thinking about that. As the miles bounced and jolted as they walked, a strange tugging on his heart got worse. Each mile they grew closer to Oregon was less time with Leah. He suddenly wished time could stand still. He was torn between wishing he'd never met her, never had a glimpse of what love could be, and longing to be the kind of man he vowed never to be—an oath breaker—and tell Molly he couldn't marry her.

There was a shout ahead, and he strained his ears for another. There was another cry, and he understood this time. The river. He, along with the other wagons, pulled up to the bank and waited, listening as the wagon master gave orders.

"One at a time you'll pull onto the raft. The ropes will be thrown to help steer you. You'll swim the team," he called loudly.

The wagons formed into a line. Stanley moved theirs into position and watched as the first wagon made the attempt.

The river was swollen, the water rushing quickly. His eyes narrowed in concern. He realized he was holding his breath, but that was all he could do, until their wagon got across and it was his turn to help man the ropes. No one had to tell them it was dangerous. They all knew it, but no one would say anything. Not mention their apprehension, or fear, or even ask to wait until the river lowered. That could take weeks, and in the meantime, another storm could come.

Stanley looked down from the wagon seat at Leah. She looked concerned, but as she met his eyes she tried to smile bravely.

He jumped down, then offered his hand. "You'll steer," he said, though she knew that. The women would sit in the seat, any children in the back of the wagon, and the men leading the teams across. It was how it was done each time.

Stanley felt his stomach drop as they grew closer. He tried to ignore that feeling. The previous wagons had made it just fine, he told himself. Still, there was a feeling that he just couldn't shake. He didn't like it. Stanley glanced up at Leah. Her face was pale, her knuckles white, and her jaw seemed to clench just a little. She must feel it too.

He told himself it was nothing. The doubt lingered though. He glanced behind him to the Jenkins' wagon. They had that same tense look. Stanley made himself relax. They were all on edge. That's all. Nothing bad was going to happen.

"Keith wagon!" someone shouted, and Stanley stepped to the front, grabbing on to the harness of the lead oxen. He stepped into the water and gasped. It was icy cold.

He didn't have to look to know Leah was watching him. He could feel her eyes on him, and it was enough to make him continue, acting as though he was calm and unworried.

"A mite cold," he called up to her, and she cracked a smile.

"I'll have a hot drink and dry clothes for you as soon as we reach the other side," she promised.

They began to cross. The oxen were fearful, and he had to soothe them as they went. The water was about one hundred yards wide. It wasn't too bad, and they could get through fairly quickly. Men who had crossed previously, along with the wagon master and scouts, pulled on the ropes connected to the raft, helping to keep it stable and moving forward, so it wouldn't go sideways and spin from the current.

Leah urged the oxen from her post in the seat, and they were about halfway across when it happened.

A rope snapped.

One moment, the wagon was making good progress. The next, one of the four ropes snapped, and the wagon shifted. Stanley felt himself forced under the water as the wagon spun. The last thing he heard before he went under the water was Leah's scream.

Chapter 10

Leah couldn't stop the scream that tore through her lips as the wagon shifted and started to go downriver. There were shouts as the men all pulled on the remaining ropes, and several others jumped into the water to try and grab the wagon from the rear.

She glanced for Stanley, but couldn't see him. A terrible fear filled her, and she called out for him. "Stanley!" There was no answer, but blessedly, the first oxen's feet hit the bank of the river right then, and the others, eager to get out of the water, followed him.

"Stanley!" Leah screamed again, dropped the reins, and half slid and half fell out of the wagon.

The men who'd jumped into the river were hauling something—no, someone—out, and set them on the bank.

It was Stanley. He was pale and had a gash in his forehead. One of the men opened his shirt and Leah spied a mass of bruises forming. He must have been hurt, possibly knocked unconscious by the wagon when it started spinning.

"He's breathing," Carl Jenkins said.

Leah looked at him in relief. She hadn't even noticed he was there. However, she spotted Claudia, who had been the wagon behind hers and had crossed on the second raft, making her way over to her. Leah accepted the other woman's embrace, and gasped into her shoulder, "What will I do?"

Claudia squeezed her tightly and gently pulled away. "What you must, my dear. Whatever that may be."

Leah nodded resolutely. "You are right," she said, and tried to hold back her tears. Whatever happened now to Stanley was in God's hands, but she wouldn't stop caring for him until the moment he either woke and recovered or...

No. She wouldn't think about that.

"Should we get him in the wagon?" Leah asked.

"Yes." Claudia turned her to her husband. "Get him out of those clothes. I'll start a fire. We'll get him warm, tend to the wounds, and go from there."

He nodded, and Leah did as well. Right. A plan. That's what she needed.

The wagon master called for a stop the rest of the day. Too many wagons had struggled getting across, and many had their supplies damaged. It would take a little time to sort through it all. Leah was grateful their supplies were dry and safe, and would have offered a hand to the others who needed it, but right now, Stanley was her concern.

In the dim light of the wagon's interior, Leah and Claudia frowned. "Could be worse," Claudia finally said. "Nothing feels broken."

"How do you know?" Leah asked. She'd watched the other woman feel all around Stanley's chest, arms, and ribs with a confidence she didn't understand.

Claudia laughed. "My husband spends a lot of time in saloons, remember? He's not one for backing down from a bar fight. If I had to call for a doctor each time, we'd have never had the funds to go West."

Leah blushed, but laughed with her friend. Times like this, one did have to laugh, didn't they? Or else cry.

"Let him rest," Claudia said, leaning back. "He's warming up, and once he's awake, you'll be able to see if he needs a poultice for his chest or not."

"Then...then you think he will wake up," Leah whispered.

Claudia reached her hand over. "I do. But I don't know when. Tomorrow, when we move out, if he's still sleeping you must drive the wagon or else they'll leave you behind. Don't worry about the oxen. I'll get you some help to unhitch them tonight and hitch them tomorrow. I'll bring you dinner tonight and the children will do any chores that need doing. You just sit with him and get what rest you can. It might be long days ahead."

Her shoulders sagging in relief, Leah said, "Thank you. Those words aren't even enough, but I appreciate you so much."

It was true. She just didn't know how she'd be able to get through the recovery of Stanley—because she refused to think it would be anything but—and also take care of all that needed to be done when it came to the team and the cooking, water and fuel gathering, and anything else that might come up.

It was a long, restless night. Stanley moved, which reassured her at first, but then Leah realized he was blazing hot. Worriedly, she set cool rags on his forehead and wrists, only to then watch him shiver. She was torn about what to do, but continued to rotate the heat and the cool, based on what he needed.

Dawn came, and she'd not done more than snooze. As the camp woke, planning to break soon, she felt panicked. Stanley was too fragile to leave as she drove the wagon, but if she didn't drive on with the train they'd be left behind.

"Leah?" Claudia's voice called at the back of the wagon.

Crawling over, Leah opened the flap to see her friend holding a mug and a bowl.

"You look terrible. You've been awake all night, I am guessing. How is he?" Claudia asked.

"Hot. Then cold," Leah said. "He's still asleep."

Claudia pressed her lips together, then nodded once. She handed Leah the dishes and called over her shoulder, "Benny. Get your pa and tell him he's got to drive for Stanley and Leah. We can't let them fall behind."

"But your wagon," Leah said, concerned.

"Will be fine for a day. The children can manage to gather enough fuel and water. I'll drive ours, and Carl will drive yours." She looked at Leah then, with a fierceness she'd never seen before. "I won't let you fall behind, Leah. You might never make it if you do."

The words chilled Leah's soul, but she knew it was true. Not a single person who fell behind could find their way on their own. Abandoned wagons attested to it, and all knew that those wagons were abandoned so the settlers could go on foot when their teams had died. The people themselves had likely perished. And it was a very real possibility that it could be her.

She couldn't answer past the lump in her throat. All Leah could do was nod, and Claudia left as quickly as she'd come, calling out to her children to make ready.

Behind her, Stanley groaned, and Leah raced to his side, one more adjusting the blankets for him.

She felt the wagon sway, and from the front of the wagon, Mr. Jenkins called out, "We're going now."

The wagon creaked and rolled, and Leah watched over Stanley. It was all she could do.

Chapter 11

Stanley wanted to talk, but his mouth and throat felt so dry it hurt. His eyes were dry and sandy feeling, but he got them open enough to see a blurry form over him.

"Molly?" he asked.

He wasn't sure why he said her name. He'd been dreaming. They'd finally reached Oregon, and Molly had been standing there waiting for him. Leah had been next to him, and he'd been holding her hand. He hadn't wanted to let it go, but Molly had started screeching at him.

"You promised," she shouted. "You promised."

"I promised you," he whispered through his dry lips. He wanted to say more, explain why he couldn't marry her, but his throat ached too badly.

"Here," a voice, coming from far away said, and then water, the best tasting thing he'd ever had in his life, touched his lips, slid down his throat, and quenched him. "Not too much," the angel said again.

He wanted more though, and strained to open his mouth. Liquid touched him again. This time a weak broth. It was heaven sent, as was the angel, he knew it. Stanley wasn't sure if that meant he was dying or healing.

"Thank you," he whispered, and closed his eyes.

Something was jostling him, making him sway. He wasn't sure what was happening, but it felt comfortable and lulled him back into drowsiness. No longer parched, he relaxed, and soon slipped into the darkness of sleep.

Chapter 12

Leah angrily wiped away a tear. Molly. He'd called her Molly. Was that how little he thought about her? On his near deathbed, and he thought about Molly. Not about her, the woman taking care of him.

She let out a sniffle, then a sob, and put her fist to her mouth. Why was she upset? She knew that's how it was. Had known it would be that way from the moment they said "I do." Stanley belonged to Molly. It didn't matter how much she was starting to get used to having him around. He wasn't hers and never had been.

"Leah? What's wrong?"

Claudia's voice startled her. Hurriedly, she wiped her tears. "Nothing," she lied. "Just tired."

Her friend shook her head and crossed her arms. "Don't you lie to me. I know you too well to see that there's something else. Won't you tell me?"

Taking a moment to consider, Leah wondered if she should. Telling someone would be a relief, but then there would also be the embarrassment of her friend knowing that her marriage to Stanley wasn't more than a temporary one.

"There's a patch of berries I spotted a short distance," Claudia continued. "Come with me and let's get a few before everyone else sees them too." She held up two mugs and Leah nodded and took one.

They walked in silence for a moment. Leah honestly didn't even know where to start.

"Is it Stanley?" Claudia asked. "Are you worried about him? He seems to be on the mend."

It was true. Today he'd sat in the wagon seat and driven the oxen. He'd tried to walk, but Leah wouldn't let him. He still needed to recover.

"A little," she admitted, sensing Claudia's look. "It's just...well, we are getting close to Oregon."

"Mmhmm?"

"Well, you see, Stanley..."

She stopped. How in the world was she to explain?

But she didn't need to. "Stanley will be off to meet the woman he is promised to," Claudia said. "Is that what you are worried about? What will happen to you?"

"A little," Leah admitted. Then, dropping a few shriveled blackberries into her cup, she said, "So you know about her?"

"I do," Claudia said. "And I also know that you and Stanley have grown close and are fond of each other." When Leah opened her mouth, Claudia continued, "And I also know that you are Stanley's wife, and she's not."

"Oh no," Leah said with a sharp laugh. "He's not interested in me at all. Matter of fact, he was calling out for her while he was sick. Over and over, he called her name. Molly. Molly. Molly." The last time, she sounded almost hysterical, and took a breath to calm herself. After a sigh, she continued, bitterness in her voice. "I was the one taking care of him, and she was the one he wanted."

Saying the words out loud made the hurts come to the surface and she hiccupped back a sob. Claudia reached and held her tightly. "My dear," she soothed. "You've no idea why that was. Why," she said, pulling back, "it could have been a nightmare."

"I doubt it," Leah said bitterly. "Pining, more like."

Claudia sighed and resumed her berry picking. "I don't know what to tell you about your marriage with Stanley. That's something the two of you have to figure out. All I can tell you is that I know he feels something for you, and it's obvious you feel something for him."

She became quiet, and Leah didn't feel the need to say anything. In the distance, several other women were approaching with mugs in hand. That was the unspoken rule in their wagon train. Never take so much others can't have any. Hence, the mugs, and not bucket, bowls, or baskets, with only a few bushes of berries.

"I can tell you this, also," Claudia said, and Leah looked at her. Her friend continued, "Once you get there, you won't be alone and left to fend for yourself. While I don't know what will happen or what fully to expect, I do know that you are always welcome wherever I am. Carl has agreed. With all we've been through together, that forms a sort of bond that one can't just ignore. We will help you figure out your way. Don't you worry about that."

"Thank you," Leah whispered, tears in her eyes. These were happy tears, though, ones of gratitude. The one thing she was grateful for about being betrayed by Jim was that she'd gotten to meet Claudia and had become friends with her.

"Let's walk back," Claudia suggested. "The others are too close for us to talk about it."

Leah nodded, and the two slowly walked toward the wagons. "I know I've no right to feel the way that I do. Jealous. But somehow, I do. For the life of me, I sure can't figure out why."

Claudia was smiling. That made Leah frown. "What's so amusing?" she asked.

"This whole thing would be so much simpler if you two would just admit how much you love each other and figure out what to do," Claudia laughed.

With a sniff, Leah said, "We don't. At least, he doesn't. And I...I don't know what I feel. Other than tired. My feet are tired, my body is tired, and my mouth is tired."

"Your mouth is tired?" Claudia looked at her, puzzled.

"Yes. Tired of bread, tired of beans, tired of salt pork, tired of oatmeal." She scowled. "I miss food. Tasty food. Fresh food."

Claudia laughed again. They were just a few feet away from their wagons. "I miss that too," she agreed. "It will be good to settle down again and have a place to buy spices and grow my own vegetables and fruits." She handed the berries to Leah. "Will you make us a cobbler for tonight?"

"I can do that," Leah agreed.

"Good. I've got to get water for washing." Claudia left, and Leah wondered if it was an excuse, as she saw Stanley approaching her.

He was tired looking, but each day he looked better. It did her heart good to see it. She'd been so worried that she might lose him. Leah took out the flour, and set to making a berry cobbler for the Jenkins, Stanley, and herself that evening as a surprise.

"Want some help?" Stanley asked.

Leah eyed him. "You can keep an eye on the beans. Stir them now and again," she said.

They sat in silence until Stanley broke it by saying, "Thank you for caring for me when I was so sick."

"Of course," she answered, stirring the flour with a little water. It didn't escape her notice that he looked like he felt uncomfortable. Awkward, even.

"I wondered...it's just. Well, are you upset at me?" Stanley asked.

Leah raised an eyebrow. "Why would you ask that? You risked your life to get us across the river safely. I'm not mad at you."

"It's not that," he agreed. "I just wonder if I did something else. You've hardly talked to me since I woke."

Leah pressed her lips together. "Is that so? I reckon I've just been tired, is all," she said.

Stanley frowned. "Is that all?" he asked. "You sure it's not something else?"

"I'm sure," Leah said, her voice tense as she poured the flour mixture over the berries and some dots of butter into a large pan she'd set in the coals. She focused on placing the lid, then stirring the beans, refusing to meet his gaze.

"Leah," he said. "Won't you look at me?"

She turned then, anger in every pore. "What is it?" she asked.

"I just want to know if you are okay," Stanley said, throwing up his hands. "I don't know why you are upset at me."

Leah put her hands on her hips. She'd not meant to say it. Not at all, but suddenly everything came bursting out. "Maybe," she hissed, not wanting to be overheard, "it's because I took care of you for days and days. And do you know the thanks I got?"

He was blinking at her, but she didn't intend to give him a chance to answer. "Molly," Leah spat. "That's what. Molly."

"Molly?" Stanley shook his head slowly. "What are you talking about?"

"I'm talking about the fact that *I* was caring for you night and day, and you kept crying out for *her*. Not for me. For her."

"Now look," Stanley said. "That's not fair. I was sick. I didn't know what I was saying."

"Your heart did, even if your mind didn't," Leah disagreed.

"My heart hasn't wanted Molly for a long time," Stanley said, raising his voice. He glanced around and saw others watching them curiously and stood, grabbing the water pail in one hand and her arm in the other. "Come on. Let's get water."

Leah was too shocked to argue and let him lead her to the stream nearby, but away from the others. Once there, he sat down the bucket and crossed his arms.

"Now why are you looking upset with me?" Leah asked, the fire within her still burning.

"Because I don't know what to do," Stanley admitted. He dropped to the ground, and rested his head in his hands. "Sit?" he asked her.

Leah bit her lip then nodded. "I can't for long, there's the cobbler," she said.

He nodded. He was so quiet she thought he wasn't going to say anything, when he finally looked over at her. "I don't love Molly. Never have. I realized that once I met you and got to know you."

Leah flicked her gaze toward him, then away again. She was pressing her lips together, determined not to interrupt.

"I knew Molly for a long time," Stanley continued. "I think it was sort of expected that we two would get married. I asked her, I guess just thinking that's what we were supposed to do." He looked off into the distance. "She said yes, her family went out West, and well, that's about it."

"But if you don't love her," Leah asked softly. "Why are you marrying her?"

Stanley shrugged. "I don't know. I told you. Obligation, I guess. I'd asked her. I need to keep my word."

That was enough. Leah stood up, hands on her hips. "Well, aren't you obligated to me as well?"

Chapter 13

A flash of anger, something he didn't often feel, flared in Stanley. He took a moment to count backward from ten, then answered calmly. "You knew this was a marriage of convenience from the start. Don't forget, I did this as a favor to you. I didn't have to marry you."

Leah flinched visibly and bit her lip. He felt guilty, but it was the truth. And it wasn't fair of her to be upset and accusing him of not meeting his obligation to her, when he already was. She opened her mouth, but he interrupted.

"The day we married, my obligation to you was to get you to Oregon. That's what I'm doing." He tried to meet her gaze, but she wasn't looking at him. "I'm sorry if that sounds harsh. But you knew that's how this was."

He stood up and shook his head. "I was trying to tell you that I felt something for you. You. Not Molly. Even was sitting here wondering what to do about that. Now, though, I see you're just the same as her. More worried about yourself than us."

Leah opened her mouth, but he turned away, leaving her behind with the water pail. She'd either fill it, or leave it empty, or leave it behind. He didn't know, and right now didn't care.

Anger fueled each step as he strode back to the camp. Claudia looked up, then over to the distance where Leah was still standing, and back at him. She kept her face neutral. For that he was grateful.

Stanley cleared his throat. "Could you keep an eye on that cobbler? Leah might be a little."

"Of course," she nodded. As he made to walk past her, Claudia stopped him with her hand on his arm. "Stanley, I don't know what's going on, and you sure don't have to tell me. But I want you to know that Leah loves you. I know Molly is waiting. Just...be gentle to Leah, won't you? She's hurting real bad. That no good man of hers let her down once, and I think she's scared you'll do the same."

Stanley shook his head. "I promised to take her to Oregon. That's what I'm doing. She knew Molly was waiting. I can't help it if she doesn't like that." Then he muttered under his breath as he walked away, "Or if I don't either."

Reaching the back of the wagon, he pulled out the sack of his personal belongings and dug through to the bundle of letters from Molly. Grabbing the most recent, he read it, glaring at each word.

Stanley. I'd like to call you dearest Stanley, but you aren't here yet. Why not? Have you forgotten all about me? Maybe found someone else? I hope not. You made me a promise.

It's been a few months since we settled here in Oregon. The weather is very different. You'll need to build us a snug house because it's much colder here. I want at least six rooms—a big kitchen and living room, three bedrooms, and then a storeroom, so that I don't have to wander outdoors if I don't want to in the winter.

Papa says that if you don't do right by me and if you don't get here soon, there's a dozen men for every woman and he can find me someone quick. Maybe even someone rich. That sounds nice. But, I'm waiting for you, like I said I would.

You had better hurry, though. I'm not going to wait forever. I'm young, pretty, and can have anyone I want. I chose you, Stanley Keith, but I can change my mind at any time.

Your soon to be wife (if you get here in time)
Molly

Stanley growled and shoved the letter back into his bag. He'd been aware of the tone when he first got the letter, that spoiled, selfish air that Molly sometimes had. But reading it again now, after being around Leah who, up until today, hadn't even demanded or asked for anything, set him on edge.

Instead of playfulness or teasing, like he'd assumed at first, with just a little of a warning or threat mixed in, he now read this for what he thought it was. Molly flat out being selfish and not caring for anyone or anything but herself.

If he had been able to join sooner, what would have happened? Likely, he'd be married already. Maybe right now, building that large house she wanted. But would it be enough? Molly's father was well off. He left for Oregon with a dozen wagons and the men to drive them. One wagon had been outfitted with plush chairs nailed down for Molly and her mother to ride in. How she survived traveling without her maid, he wondered. But she had. And was just as spoiled and demanding as ever.

Maybe that's why Leah had made him so upset. But Claudia's words to him echoed, and he stiffened. He hoped he hadn't given Leah cause to worry about her safety or getting to Oregon. He was nothing like that man, Jim.

The sound of footsteps startled him, and he turned to see Leah. She was looking at her shoes. When she stopped, she looked up and whispered, "I'm sorry. You are right. I..." she swallowed hard. "I have no right at all for any expectations from you. You have no obligation to me. I just...we were...and I forgot that we...even though we hadn't..." She stopped, her cheeks a bright red.

Stanley moved toward her and stood close. When she glanced up at him, he cupped her face in his hands and kissed her. The world seemed to stop, and all there was were the two of them. A sudden shout from the distance startled them, and they broke apart. Leah's eyes were wide and her cheeks pink as she looked at him.

He ran a hand through his hair. "I shouldn't have done that," he muttered. At her flash of disappointment, he added, "Kiss you without asking, I mean."

A tiny smile formed. "You can kiss me any time you like," Leah said shyly. "It was a nice kiss. The best I've ever had."

Stanley pulled her close and felt her relax against him. "What are we going to do?" he whispered. "I don't want Molly. I want you."

There was a soft sigh from Leah, and she looked up at him. "When you were pulled out of the river, you were pale, and bruised and bleeding. I was terrified. I didn't know what to do."

He wasn't sure where she was going with this and looked at her in confusion. "Go on?"

Leah took a deep breath and rested her head against his chest. "I asked the same thing. And Claudia said I needed to do what I must. Whatever that may be." She pulled back enough to meet his eyes. "That's what we'll both do. Whatever we must. Right now," she closed her eyes and a sob escaped from her lips, "that's you must talk with

Molly. If she still wants you for her husband, that's what you promised. And I promised that I was okay with that."

As a tear rolled down her cheek, Stanley caught it on his finger. "You are more wonderful than you know," he said. He pressed his lips to the top of her head. "I don't know what will happen. But I do know that I'm always going to be in love with you."

Leah's smile was enormous as she looked up at him. His head lowered, and breathed her in, smelling the rose-scented soap she was carefully rationing. He was about to kiss her once more when a foreign smell entered his nose. One of smoke. It was enough to startle him. The short hairs on the back of his neck rose and he tensed. A moment later, shouts filled the air.

"Prairie fire!"

Chapter 14

Leah gasped and looked around, confused. "Stanley?" she asked.

He was looking concerned, and stood on the wagon to get a better look. "Oh no," he gasped. "This isn't good."

All around them, men and women were rushing to the wagons and pulling out tools. Children were rushing to the stream, the older ones holding the small ones in the water, while those large enough to help were grabbing buckets to fill with water.

"I don't understand," Leah said, as Stanley pulled out a shovel and some sacks. "What's happening?"

He pointed to the distance, where a near endless line of smoke filled the air. "Fire. We won't outrun it. When a prairie fire starts, it spreads fast. All we can do is try to prevent it from getting any closer." He pointed to a few dozen feet away, where men were starting to dig a trench. "We need to make a barrier, one deep enough and wide enough the fire can't cross."

Leah felt cold then. That's why the youngest children were in the water. It was to save their lives. She grabbed two buckets. "I'll fill these with water and start wetting the ground," she said, knowing that it wouldn't help much but unable to think of how else she could help.

"I've got a plow!" Carl shouted then, waving his arms for attention. "I need to clear the wagon to get it. It's near the back. I'll make a furrow."

Women clustered around his wagon, making a line as item by item things were pulled from the wagon and heaped on the ground so Carl and Stanley could get the plow. Meanwhile, Claudia unhitched the oxen and readied one to pull the plow.

Hurriedly, Carl started, shouting at his ox to go faster as a patch of ground turned over. Leah watched, frozen to the spot, as the wall of smoke grew closer. "Don't just watch," Claudia said urgently, and handed her a bucket. "Let's wet the ground."

A line of women and older children had formed from the wagons to the stream, and buckets were being passed back and forth. The men were working hard, digging and scraping away the prairie grasses, throwing them away from the dirt Carl was pulling up. It would do no good for him to plow a circle of safety for them, if the dried grass was still there, and an easy way for the fire to spread.

The smoke now stung their eyes. Leah coughed, her eyes watered as they ached, but she didn't stop passing buckets. As one, the women worked, as did the men. Carl moved closer to the fire, trying to make a second, further away fire break.

"Wet the middle!" the wagon master shouted, and the women shifted their line so the buckets of water would go in the strip of grass between the two lines. That would help reduce the fire's chance of going over the fire break, and any sparks that flew might be dampened and put out.

"He's too close," Claudia whispered, and Leah looked at her friend. Tears were running down her cheeks. Soot on her face washed away in two tiny trails.

"Your husband is a hero," Leah said, taking a moment to squeeze her friend's hand. "He just might save us all."

Claudia nodded, straightened her shoulders, and grabbed the bucket offered to her, passing it along to the next woman.

"Fall back! Get to the water!" the wagon master yelled, waving at the women. "Hurry! Hurry!" He called to the men, "Fall back!"

The heat from the flames drew close, and Leah felt sweat form over every inch of her. The fire seared her and it felt like her flesh was going to melt off. She turned, anxious to get away from the roaring inferno.

The women headed to the water, but not all of the men did. Carl kept plowing. Leah couldn't even see him, the smoke was so thick. Claudia shook with silent sobs, and Leah wrapped her arms around her as the Jenkins children huddled about them.

"I don't think it's coming any closer," a woman said suddenly, in a hopeful tone.

"Praise God!" another gasped.

The smoke was so thick now, Leah couldn't see anything. Shadows were running toward the water, and she assumed they were the men. *Please, let Stanley, and Carl, and everyone else be okay,* she prayed.

There was a splashing sound as people entered the water. "Hold your sleeves to your nose," Leah said to the children clinging to her, helping the smallest ones nearby.

"It's working!" The wagon master's familiar voice sounded loudly, and Leah felt a surge of relief. It was true. The scorching heat of the flames had receded. The smoke was lessening.

"Stanley?" Leah called.

All around her, women were calling to their husbands. In the confusion, she was sure he wouldn't hear her. She ventured forward a step and felt a familiar hand in hers.

"Leah? Are you hurt?"

She turned and flung herself at Stanley. "I'm fine. I'm fine." She pulled back and searched him with her eyes. He looked exhausted, and his skin was covered in more soot than flesh. His shirt had a few charred spots on it. She imagined she also looked a fright. "What of you?" she asked.

"Tired," he said. "But not hurt."

They embraced, and Leah looked over to see Claudia and Carl doing the same. Her shoulders sagged in relief. "He's alive! He may have saved us all," she said.

"No may about it," Stanley said, shaking his head. "He did. None of us would be here had it not been for Carl staying so long."

They walked over, and Stanley clapped Carl on the back. "I'm your man, any time you need one. You saved me and Leah, and everyone else here. It's a debt I can't ever repay, but I'll never stop trying."

Carl looked a little embarrassed, and shrugged, "Just had the right tool for the job, is all."

"Was more than that," the wagon master said, coming closer. "You stayed behind and didn't stop plowing. Saved every one of us."

Cheers broke out, and Leah was jostled as everyone tried to get close and shake Carl's hand, pat him on the back, or offer their debts of gratitude.

Stanley led her a short distance to the side, to where the children all stood in the water, unsure if they could get out or not. He winked at them, and said, "I've a sack of candy in my wagon, and a piece for each of you, if you want it?"

Delighted gasps and big smiles formed on the small faces. A few of the older children stood shyly off to the side. They had been ones manning sacks and buckets of water.

"You too," Stanley said. "Don't think I don't know how hard you worked as well!"

As their smiles got bigger, and the troupe of children followed Stanley to their wagon, Leah hung back a moment smiling. He was wonderful with children. Would they ever have any of their own?

But as soon as the thought sprang to mind, she remembered. There was a barrier to their happiness. Molly.

Chapter 15

Stanley glanced over at Leah in the wagon seat next to him. When she met his gaze, she smiled, which made his heart flutter like nobody's business.

They were both riding today. With the majority of their supplies used up, they sat together on occasion, deciding that a few hours a day, the oxen would be fine with the extra load.

"Look at those mountains," Leah murmured.

"I've never seen anything like them," Stanley said. "They rise up taller than I think anyone could climb them."

"Not without a lot of help," Leah agreed. "Too high for me. I think I might get dizzy."

"I read once that the higher up you go, the harder it is to breathe. I expect it would make a lot of us dizzy," Stanley said.

"What do you read?" Leah asked.

He tore his gaze from the large green mounds in the distance, some of the peaks rising up so high he was sure they blocked the sun early each day. The tops were a different color, and Stanley wondered if there was snow on them. He'd also read that to see snow on the mountaintops, even in summer, wasn't unusual.

"I'll read about anything I can get my hands on," Stanley told her. He grinned. "Might be a little strange, but I feel like a man—or woman—can't know too much. There's a lot to learn, and I suspect I'll never have a chance to learn all of it, but I'm sure going to try. You never know when something you read about will come in handy."

"I agree," Leah said. Then she looked at him shyly. "I also like reading. Jim told me—" she stopped, and looked down at her hands.

Stanley reached over and covered her hands with one of his. "Whatever he told you was likely wrong," he said. "Just so you know."

The grateful look she flashed at him didn't go unnoticed. She cleared her throat and said, "He told me that women shouldn't try to be too clever. That men didn't like that. And it would make it hard to find someone. He also said that's why I was so lucky to have him. He was willing to overlook my faults."

Stanley clenched his jaw and opened his mouth, but before he could say anything, her giggle caught him off guard. "What's so funny?" he asked.

"Just remembering something," Leah said, as her giggles grew and tears of mirth formed in her eyes. "I later found out he couldn't even read. So, no wonder he didn't want me reading. It was the silliest thing too. I'd bought some sweets in a tin. When I offered him one, he got upset at me. Said why was I offering him soap to eat."

"Soap?"

She nodded and giggled. "Yes. I never understood why he thought that's what I was doing, and of course, I pretended I didn't hear him and pulled off the lid."

Stanley shook his head. "I still don't understand why you stepped out with a person like that."

Leah was quiet a moment, all trace of her humor gone. Finally, she said, "It's because when you don't have anyone else, you tend to follow the first person who makes you feel good about yourself some of the time, even if you know it's maybe not a good idea."

"That's behind you now," Stanley said. "And from this day forward, I want you to know something." She looked at him, and he made sure to fix his eyes on hers. "You are worthy of whoever you choose. More than. You are also clever, and that's a good thing. You're a fine woman, in more ways than I could possibly count. I've felt grateful to have this time with you."

Leah leaned her head on his shoulder. "Can you promise me something?" she asked, her voice small.

"I can try," he answered.

"Let's still be friends. I don't...I don't ever want to not have you in my life some way."

"That, I can do," Stanley said, and wrapped one arm around Leah.

They rode in silence, neither of them wanting to have a dose of reality by thinking too much. Stanley let his gaze roam from Leah's sweet face to the mountains, to the wagon just in front and to the left of them. It was the Perkins wagon. The newlyweds just had their first baby.

Stanley wondered, what would it be like to have his own family? Little ones crowded at his knee, in his arms. He could teach his boys how to ride horses and make things. His daughters he would carve dolls for and swing them in his arms. On Sunday afternoons, the family would picnic on the bank by a stream. There Leah would read to them, in her sweet voice—

Leah. The thought of her name shook him to his core. If somehow he could figure this out, if he and Molly didn't marry, would Leah ever want to have a family with him?

But perhaps a more important question was, once she got to Oregon and saw those dozen men for every one woman that Molly claimed, and he didn't doubt they existed, would she ever want someone like him?

Chapter 16

"We're almost there," Claudia sighed happily. "All this walking will be done soon. No more sleeping in a wagon. Carl's promised first thing, he'll get us proper beds."

"I can't wait," Leah sighed. "I never want to eat another bowl of beans again. Or salt pork."

Claudia laughed. "I understand. I'm getting tired of them too."

"There's something I'm not sure on," Leah said. "You know when we get there Stanley is duty bound to go to Molly. I don't know what will happen and I'm not going to even let myself think about it," Leah said, drawing in a deep breath. "But I need help. I'm not sure how to stake a claim, and I likely won't have Stanley to ask and help me."

"Don't you worry," Claudia assured her. "I don't either, but you and I will go to the claim office with Carl, and he'll help you. We'll figure out everything that you need to do, together."

"I appreciate that," Leah said with a sigh of relief. "I couldn't do this without you."

"Oh, you could," Claudia disagreed. "But there's no need for you to. We're almost family, you know. Whatever you need, we will help with."

Leah couldn't answer past the lump in her throat, but she knew she didn't need to. Claudia understood, because her own eyes had tears in them.

"I've grown so used to you being here," Leah admitted suddenly. "I don't quite know if I'll be able to manage on my own. You see, in the boarding house, someone else did the cooking, I didn't really have cleaning to do. Just my laundry. The idea of trying to figure this all out, to even do whatever I need to do to one day build my own home... I'm not sure if I can even do all of that."

With a sigh, Leah added, "It's also not just you. It's Stanley. I keep worrying about how I'm going to get along without him. I know this was supposed to be just a marriage of convenience. Neither Stanley nor I expected anything different. Somehow, though, I've fallen in love with him and it breaks my heart knowing that I have to say goodbye."

She turned a worried gaze to Claudia. "What if I can't do any of it right? There's a lot to do, being on your own in a place this wild. Even if I live in town. It's filled with strangers. What will they be like? What if the money I have won't get me very far? I had to leave in such a rush."

"I'm sure what you have will be a start, and we won't let you starve," Claudia assured her. "There's some civilization there, even if it's less than we had back in the East. They'll be good people, and we will look for them. You'll be safe, I'm sure. If you don't feel safe, you'll stay with us. I expect you can find some work somewhere too."

"Honest work, I hope," Leah said. "I don't need my reputation at risk again."

"I'm here to help," Claudia promised. "I'm not going to let anyone make up stories about you." She stopped then, and threw her arms around Leah. "It's going to work out. Don't you worry."

Leah returned the embrace, feeling better. Claudia was right. She wasn't alone. The last few months she'd made such a good friend in both Stanley and Claudia, and she was sure that if she really needed help, they would assist.

As they pulled apart, Leah smiled. "Thank you. I feel better. Well," she laughed, "my heart does. My feet? Hurting. I want to sit for a week straight when we get there."

"Me too," Claudia sighed. "I thought they were joshing when they said we'd wear out two pairs of shoes. I'm on my last pair, and it's getting a hole."

"Look at my boot toe!" Stanley called, as he rode up to them. He waved his foot in the air, and the women laughed to see the toe leather flapping.

"When did that happen?" Leah asked.

"This morning," he told her. "I'll have a breeze for my feet until we get there."

"Make camp!" the wagon master called. "We arrive tomorrow!"

There were excited shouts and cheers from the settlers. Stanley jumped down from the wagon, picked Leah up, and spun her around. "We've made it!" he said with a grin. Leah's heart felt light. Somehow, she felt confident they'd get there and everything would turn out just fine.

Then she and Stanley looked at each other. Reality sunk in. They'd made it...this was the end. Leah bit her lip and nodded, forcing a smile. "Thank you for getting me here safely," she said.

His eyes searched hers for so long Leah could hardly breathe. There seemed to be something he wanted to say. She knew there was a great deal she wanted to say, however, also knew she couldn't.

Finally, he leaned in closely, his lips dangerously close to hers, and whispered, "I promised."

"You did," she answered softly, reaching for his hands.

Neither of them said anything else. In fact, the rest of the day was spent in near silence.

That night, it was hard for the camp to settle. The fact that their long journey was nearly at an end was exciting for nearly everyone there. Children, who couldn't remember what a town looked like by now, were full of questions for their parents. Leah couldn't help but smile as the Jenkins children were almost bouncing around.

As the stars filled the open skies and campfires were extinguished, Leah realized she was exhausted. Whether it was from their long journey, or from the emotions she'd had to bottle up, she wasn't sure.

She crawled into the back of the wagon, in her usual spot. The wagon seat creaked as Stanley sat down. Leah laid there a moment, and then sat up, climbing through the canvas cover at the front of the wagon to where Stanley was staring up at the moon.

"You okay?" he whispered, sitting up.

Leah hesitated, then nodded. "Yes. No. But I decided, if this is our last night out here together, and some of our last hours, I'm not going to waste a moment of it." She sat next to him and joined in looking upward.

"Leah," he whispered. "I'm sorry."

She took in a shuddering breath. "So am I," she answered softly.

Their hands met, their fingers laced, and Leah rested her head against Stanley's shoulder. When tomorrow came, she couldn't say goodbye. Wouldn't. It would be too hard. Too painful. Leah hoped he'd understand.

As if he knew that she was thinking about the future that had to come, he whispered. "Everything will work out." Those words played around and around in her mind for a while.

Though Leah knew the words were meant to bring comfort, she had the feeling nothing could have been further from the truth.

The last several months had been filled with hardships and loss. Not everyone they'd started out with had made it. Some, like Stanley, nearly died. She craved security and stability. Would Oregon provide it, or would it be filled with more difficulties, and now, she'd have to face them alone?

Chapter 17

Stanley glanced over his shoulder. There was a pain in his chest. An ache, a hollow, but it wasn't any sickness. It was from missing Leah.

The day had been too rushed. They'd traveled a short distance and arrived at their final destination, a small town called Surrey. When they'd pulled up, the wagon master grunted. "Wasn't named this last time," he said, making a note on his map. "Wonder if it will change on my next trip."

The fact that small towns did change their names at times was confusing, to be sure. Stanley luckily had directions to Molly's parents' home. They'd been left for him at the post office. He'd sent a note right away, paying someone to take it to them, saying he had arrived.

As he held the paper with their location in his hands, he couldn't help but feel reluctant to find her. His feet didn't want to move. It wasn't just that his legs were tired. There was a general feeling of unease. It was likely to be expected, not having seen her for so long. But where he should have felt at least a little excited, he felt nothing.

That morning, the preacher on the wagon train who'd wed him and Leah, had asked quietly if they were sure this was what they wanted. With their quiet nods, the preacher wrote a letter as testament that Stanley and Leah had entered into a marriage of convenience only, and after the three signed it, promised to see it delivered to a judge so their annulment could go through.

He was no longer a married man. That is, until Molly got a ring on him.

Stanley sighed, then pulled on his new boots. The general store there was huge, bigger than anything he'd ever seen, and it was well stocked, like they knew the wagon train settlers would need all manner of supplies. He'd bought himself a new pair of boots, a new shirt and pants, and even a new hat. He felt extravagant getting the hat, but you couldn't go ask a woman for her hand in marriage looking as filthy as he had when they'd first arrived.

Keeping clean on the Oregon trail was difficult. There was hardly enough water to drink, let alone wash with. Though there were no complaints by anyone, he was sure there wasn't a man, woman, or child who wasn't looking forward to a proper bath.

Stanley looked over his shoulder again, hoping he'd see Leah. He didn't. She'd left with the Jenkins for the land office that morning, finding out what they needed to do to stake a claim.

Going to the livery, he paid handsomely to borrow a horse. "You familiar with Ted Shaw's place?" he asked the owner.

The man spit. "I am. What business do you have there?"

That wasn't the sort of answer he'd expected. "Uh, business with his daughter," Stanley answered. "We were planning to get married."

The man squinted at him, and then laughed. "Good luck," he said. Then he pointed. "Ride down that way. About five miles. Big house. You can't miss it. Biggest place around."

"Thanks," Stanley said. He swung up on the horse and set out. As he was leaving town, there was a flash of yellow that went into the general store. For a moment, he thought about Leah, and the first time he'd seen her in that yellow dress.

What was she doing now? Would she be okay by herself? Okay without him? And would he be okay without her? Logically, the answer should be yes, he'd be fine. But he just didn't think that would be the case. Not really.

Stanley rode the mare in the direction he'd been told, and tried to take in the scenery, not get lost in his worries.

Oregon was stunning. There was no other word for it. Tall mountains of greens and purples and blues rode in the distance. He'd never seen such colors in nature, nor anything so majestic. Overhead, large birds flew, a field of grain waved, and the distant sound of the town behind him made his heart feel lighter.

A man could get used to a place like this. It would be better with Leah at his side, no doubt, but that wasn't something he could have, even if he'd told her things would work out. They both knew it was a lie. But neither of them were going to tell the other they knew it wasn't real.

The Shaw place appeared suddenly, a large house almost out of nowhere. He whistled low as he rode in. The Shaws were well off, and by the looks of this two-story house that was bigger than some of the mansions he'd seen back East, they weren't going to let anyone forget that fact.

He slowed to a walk and looked around as he got closer. It was quiet. There wasn't anyone around. Were they home? He wasn't sure, but only one way to find out.

Stanley dismounted and then hitched the mare. He walked to the front door and knocked.

From within, he could hear footsteps. The door opened suddenly, and there he was, face to face with Molly.

Chapter 18

Leah yawned and stretched. She really didn't want to leave the comfort of the boarding house. Though Claudia had offered to let her stay with them in their wagon, she'd had enough and was more than grateful to find a room at a fair price that included two meals daily and a hot bath.

A bath! Such luxury! A dreamy smile stretched across her face as she thought back to it. First, the steaming water. Ahh! She soaked away aches that had been building over months. A proper shampoo and time to relax had been quite restorative, and practically made her feel like a new woman.

An unmarried woman, which would take getting used to, but a new woman all the same. Leah turned her head toward the window. She wondered what Stanley was doing right now. He was likely with Molly. The very thought made her heart sink and her stomach hurt.

It had only been a day since they'd said goodbye. It had been short. Quiet. Difficult. Already she was wondering how she'd manage without him.

Taking a deep breath, Leah threw back the blankets and rose. She got dressed quickly. Today, her goal was to find work. After visiting the land office with Claudia and Carl, she'd determined that the stipulations to own land might be more than she was ready for. She could claim land, but then she'd have to live on it for years before it could be considered her own. Claudia had begged her to reconsider, showed that they could get land near each other, but Leah wasn't sure.

Claudia and Carl would have enough to do to build their own place. They couldn't be helping her, and where was she to live in the meantime? No, she wasn't the sort to settle just yet, not without a plan. And that's just what she hoped to formulate. In the meantime, though, she had to have more funds.

After getting dressed, Leah ate fluffy biscuits covered in jam, two pieces of bacon, and a small bowl of oatmeal in the dining room with the other boarders, then made her way out to the town.

It wasn't the largest, not as big as where she'd come from, but there was a friendly feel here. Leah turned her head slowly for a moment, considering which place to try first. There was a butcher, a baker, the general store, a dressmaker, a restaurant. Also the town had a bank, a doctor, a barber, and the boarding house. She was sure there was more, but that was all she saw from her vantage point.

Seeing as the general store also boasted the post office, Leah decided to start there. The largest building in town, it might also be the most likely to offer employment. Crossing the dusty street, Leah pushed open the door, a sturdy one with a glass panel near the top, and walked inside.

A small bell had signaled her entry, and an older couple looked up, smiles on their faces.

"Hello," the woman said first. "Welcome. How can I help you?"

Leah drew closer, even though she longed to browse the shelves. It had been far too long since she'd been in a store. It was almost overwhelming. Bolts of fabric in beautiful colors begged her to run her fingers over them. Smells from spices galore assaulted her nose and made her flavor-starved mouth water.

Almost reluctantly, she pulled her eyes away from the shelf of books and a basket of scented soaps and walked toward the couple. "Hello," she answered. "I am new here. I was wondering if you might be hiring someone to help in your store?"

"I don't know," the man answered. Then he added, "I'm Louis Smith, this is Ellie, my wife. We own the store and run the post office."

After Leah nodded her hello, she said, "Back home, I worked in the post office for two years before coming on the Oregon Trail."

"Is that so?" Louis answered. "We get a lot of mail. Might could use a hand."

"Today's just came in," Ellie said. "Why don't you let us watch you sort it?"

Feeling just a little nervous, Leah stepped closer. They opened the sack and set the mail in front of her. There must have been over a hundred letters.

"A lot of folks write here, knowing it's the final destination for many," Louis explained. "We sort by alphabetical, for that reason. Many new folks, so no set slot for any of them."

He motioned to a wall of cubbies, and Leah looked at it quickly, then nodded. "I can do this," she said, and set to work. She picked up a handful of the letters and started to shelve them, working the folded papers and envelopes into the correct order. She was so lost in her movements, she didn't realize she was done until she reached for the last stack and found the counter bare.

Ellie came over and sorted through the cubbies at random, and then stepped back with a nod of satisfaction.

"Well done. And faster than I can do it, with my eyes. You've a job, if you want one."

"Oh yes," Leah said. "Thank you."

"We've a room above," Louis continued. "Separate entrance. Yours, if you want it. Unless, that is, you've a husband."

This was almost more than she could imagine. At their look of waiting expectation, Leah's throat grew tight. "I'd be grateful for the room," she told them. "And no, I am not married anymore."

The couple traded sympathetic looks, but Leah didn't want to take the time to explain, nor did she desire to. Really, who would want to be thought of as the woman who was so undesirable that her marriage of convenience didn't even last? Why, even a mail-order bride couldn't say that!

"Can you start tomorrow?" Louis asked. "You can move in then, as well. Has a stove, a bed, and chair. Not much else, but it's clean."

"It sounds perfect, and yes, I can," Leah assured him.

She thanked him and Ellie, then left, a weight of worry lifted from her shoulders. Work meant income. It was a stroke of luck getting to have a place of her own too. Even if it was a small room, she wouldn't care. A stove meant she could cook, as well. It was a wonderful blessing and an excellent start to her new adventure.

Leah decided to stroll through the town and get acquainted with it. After all, it was home now. She stopped in the bakery and bought herself an apple muffin to celebrate her new job, then found a bench overlooking a small stream. As she sat eating her muffin, the water reminded her of the place she used to meet Jim at.

With a small smile, Leah wondered if he'd even recognize her now. She'd grown so much over the last few months she'd hardly recognize herself. No longer did she let everyone tell her what to do. She didn't let anyone tell her what to wear or who to talk to. Having grown up with a demanding mother, and then a step father who forced her out very quickly, she had become used to people not giving her any options of choices in her own life.

Was that why Jim's treatment of her hadn't seemed unusual? She pondered this question as she took a bite of her nearly finished muffin. A hint of cinnamon hit her tongue and she was determined to buy herself another one soon.

With Jim, she had enjoyed that feeling of protection he provided at first. Only now, she realized he wasn't protecting her. He was isolating her. Everything he did and said had one purpose, and that was to make her dependent on him and pull her away from anyone who could help her if she needed it.

And when she did need help, it had worked. There wasn't a soul in town who would risk being associated with a compromised woman. Had the wagon train not been there, and had Stanley not offered to marry her...well, things would be very different. It wasn't something she wanted to think about.

Now, she had choices, and friends, and confidence. She had a new job, a new home, and...heartache. Leah wiped away a tear that had sprung up out of nowhere. She missed Stanley. How long would it take before that hole in her heart filled?

With a sigh, she ate the last bite of muffin, put the brown paper it had been wrapped in into her handbag, and rose.

Turning back toward the town, Leah took one last look at the small stream and straightened her shoulders a little more. Yes. Old Leah was gone. This new Leah, formed from hundreds of miles of walking, the learning of new skills, and the confidence and love given to her by strangers, was feeling determined.

Determined to move forward with her life, even if she didn't have Stanley in it. Determined to make the best of her situation. Determined to leave her heartache behind.

At least, she hoped she could believe that lie. Living without Stanley would be much harder than just about anything, she suspected.

Chapter 19

"What took you so long?" Molly stood in front of Stanley, her arms crossed over her chest. There was no welcoming smile. No affection in the form of a hug. No tears of joy. He hadn't expected those, to be honest. But a hello, a smile, that he had.

"Hello, Molly," he answered. "My journey was long. Not as easy as yours, in a caravan of my pa's wagons, with a plush chair and the comforts of home. Had to work to get here. Arrived yesterday," he continued, unwilling to hide the sarcasm in his voice. "Glad to have a warm welcome."

She pressed her lips together and Stanley took a moment to look at her. Nearly as tall as he was, she was dressed in a pale blue dress with more ruffles than he'd ever seen. Her blonde hair was curled and a ribbon was holding part of it away from her face.

Molly took a dramatic pose. "You have no idea how difficult the journey was," she sighed. "All that riding. And if you didn't sit, you walked. You don't want to know what we had to burn for fuel," she added, with a shudder. "And goodness, near the end we had to ration our tea to just three cups a day." She shook her head then, and the blonde curls trembled. "It was so uncivilized."

"That'll change quick," Stanley said, staring off into the distance. "I expect things will keep growing, people keep coming. It will be easier one day to make the journey to and from the West and East."

"Right you are, my boy," Molly's father boomed, as he came around the side of the house. "Good to see you, Stanley. Wasn't expecting you."

Stanley wondered if he looked as surprised as he felt. "You weren't? I sent a note when we pulled in yesterday."

Mr. Shaw shook his head. "Well, come on inside. Let's get you a cool drink." He looked at Molly. "You told him yet?"

"Told me what?" Stanley asked, stepping onto the porch. His eyes flicked between Molly and her father. Molly was nearly squirming.

Mr. Shaw sighed as he caught sight of Molly's movements. "You didn't." He faced Stanley then. "My boy, I'm sorry. Molly wasn't sure you were coming. Neither were we. She's had one gentleman after another trying to take her hand in marriage."

"And?" Stanley shoved his hands into his pockets. If he didn't, he wasn't exactly sure what he was going to do with them, but a flicker of anger was forming. He'd been true to Molly. Kept his word. Had she?

"I'm getting married next week," Molly said, her chin raised. "Not to you, though. He owns a hotel chain. Making one the next town over. That's where we'll live."

Stanley took a step back without realizing it. "You..." He stopped.

It felt like someone had punched him in the gut. Here he'd been thinking about her since the day they parted. The whole trip here, he'd thought about his obligation to her. All that time he had wasted with Leah. All the hurt he'd caused her. Every bit of it over Molly. Molly, who didn't care at all. Not for him, anyway. She only cared about herself. That much was obvious. He and Leah could have started a life together. Could be together right now!

Stanley blew out a breath of anger and rubbed a hand through his hair. "I thought we were waiting for each other," he said, still filled with disbelief.

Never mind a small part of him was excited he was free. A larger part had the feeling he'd lost Leah, and there was no getting her back. He didn't know where she was. Didn't know if he could ever make amends for this.

Molly shrugged, and her casualness made him near boil over with anger. He looked away, then back at her. Her father had stepped a short distance away to give them privacy, but he was still listening.

Stanley wanted to say something more. But he wasn't sure what. It came to him then, each moment that he wasted was another moment more that Leah might be getting away from him.

With a nod, Stanley turned and started to walk away.

"Don't you cause any trouble," Molly's shrill voice called from behind him.

Stanley turned and took his hat off, holding it in front of him and giving her a sweeping bow. "Wouldn't dream of it," he said. "I've always kept my word. Goodbye, Molly. Mr. Shaw."

He mounted the horse and rode back toward town, faster than he'd left it. The horse's hooves struck the path and inside of his mind, a single name echoed in his thundering heart.

Leah.

Leah.

Leah.

When he got to town, he headed right to the land office. Dismounting, he tied his horse and rushed in. The clerk looked up at him from behind a desk stacked high with papers.

"Carl Jenkins," Stanley said. "Where's his land?"

"Well, let's see here," the man said. He stood and walked over to a large book. Slowly, he began to turn the pages.

"Jenkins," he muttered. "Let's see. Franklin, no, not far enough. James, closer. Kennedy, too far."

Stanley waited impatiently. "Well?" he finally asked, as the man stood quietly, running his finger down a column of names.

The clerk went to a map hanging on the wall and tapped. "Thereabouts," he told him.

Stanley went over and stared at the map for a long moment, fixing it in his mind. He had to find them. If anyone knew where Leah was, it would be Claudia. With some luck, she would even be there with the Jenkins.

"Thank you," he said, hurrying back out to the horse.

Once again, Stanley rode out of town, and about two hours later, parched and tired, with the sun about to set, he spotted a covered wagon in the distance. As he got closer, a familiar woman waved her hand at him. Stanley came to a stop. "Claudia," he said. "Where's Leah?"

She gave him a puzzled look. "Why are you here? What about your intended?" Then she squinted at him. "You look exhausted. Here. I have some ginger water."

Stanley followed her to the water bucket and eagerly drank. "Any water for my horse?" he asked.

"Of course," she said. "Trough over there."

He led the horse in the direction Claudia pointed, then he turned to find her watching him. "Where's Leah?" he asked again.

"She's not here," Claudia said softly.

Stanley gripped the edge of the trough. A sick feeling washed over him as his worst fear came to life. He was too late. Leah wasn't there, and he didn't know where she was.

"Claudia," he whispered. "Molly's found someone else. I want to find Leah. To apologize. To...to..." he stopped then. To what? He wasn't fully sure. There wasn't a plan, not really. He just knew that he wanted her back.

"Well," Claudia said with a smile. "I know where she is."

Chapter 20

It had only been three days since she had arrived, but Leah was feeling quite settled in. It was comforting at night, being surrounded by four walls. Sleeping in the open air wasn't something she'd gotten used to. A door between her and any danger was such comfort she really didn't want to get out of bed each morning.

Today, however, was her first day downstairs in the general store at the post office. Ellie had asked if she would manage the post alongside her, and also learn how to run the counter. Leah was quite excited. She was even more delighted to know that she'd soon be surrounded by all of those wonderful items filling the store, and with the money to buy some of them for herself.

After dressing, Leah cut a small wedge of cheese and placed it on a slice of bread, then ate while the kettle boiled.

Ellie had loaned her a few kitchen items, and Leah fully intended to buy her own as soon as possible.

Ready to start work, she headed downstairs and got started on the stack of mail. As she sorted, Ellie walked in and greeted her on her way to open the store. Leah found the sorting of the mail soothing. There was a calming rhythm to it.

One by one, the letters were alphabetized. Mille Jacobs. Anna Lindy. Jeff Dawson. Stanley—Stanley? Her heart leaped, and her stomach jolted. Then she took a shuddering breath. Stanley Mason. Not Stanley Keith.

Leah filed the letter in the correct position. No, Stanley Keith was off, wherever he was. With Molly. She wondered briefly how he was. That's all she'd allow herself—a short moment here and there. Her heart couldn't take more than that. Would Molly ever come in here to shop? Would Stanley? And if so, could she bear it?

Tears threatened to form, and Leah firmly pushed them aside. It was time to move forward with her new life. Not the old.

Hours passed quicker than she could have imagined. It was enjoyable being in the store. It was near lunch time, and Leah was looking forward to her break. One of those apple muffins from the bakery sounded quite tasty. She held back a yawn. Once Ellie had returned from her lunch, she could go.

The door opened, and the small bell rang. "Welcome," Louis called from a stack of dry goods he was inventorying.

"Hello."

Leah's head snapped up. It was Stanley. She didn't know if she should stare or hide or—it was too late. He'd spotted her, and stepped forward with urgency.

"Leah," he said, and his single word was music to her ears. "Can I speak with you for a few moments?"

"Who is this?" Ellie asked, as she came down the stairs. She looked him up and down, but Leah didn't know her well enough to know what kind of expression she had.

"We were together on the wagon train," Leah said. "Mr. Keith was a huge help."

"Ah," Louis said. "Well, you are due for your lunch. Go ahead. Back in a half hour for the afternoon mail, please."

"Yes, of course," Leah said, and stepped from behind the counter. "Thank you."

Stanley nodded at Louis and Ellie, then opened the door for Leah. They'd hardly gotten outside when he said, "I've been looking for you."

"Have you?" Leah tried not to sound too happy at his words. After all, it was likely he wanted her for something simple. Like he'd misplaced something.

"I have," he said. "I want to talk to you. If you'll listen."

"I will," Leah said softly. Then she looked up. "But I hope you don't mind. I'm terribly hungry and if I don't eat now, it will be a very long time before I can. How about I get us something from the bakery?"

"That sounds good," Stanley agreed. "I'm hungry too. Claudia gave me breakfast—"

"Claudia! How is she?" Leah asked eagerly.

"She's fine," Stanley said, opening the bakery door. "She's who told me where you were."

Leah nodded, and waited by the glass counter. When the baker walked over, she said, "I'll have an apple muffin, please."

"Make that four," Stanley said. "Those rolls over there too, and some butter for them, please. We are taking them with us." He set out money, and at Leah's protest said, "Please. Let me."

She nodded, and when the baker had given Stanley the order, held the door for him.

"There's a bench nearby," Leah said. "We don't have time for me to go too far."

Stanley nodded. They went to the bench, and he handed Leah a roll with butter spread in the middle. They ate in silence and she wondered what he wanted to talk about. When she'd finished her roll, Stanley offered her another.

"No, thank you. Their muffins are incredibly good. Let's have those now." She smiled at him and reached in the bag for two. Stanley's eyes widened at his bite. "I know," she agreed, with a small laugh.

It felt good to sit here with him. Normal. Right. Comfortable. She could go on and on. In fact, Leah suspected the dictionary she'd put out for sale this morning would be chock full of words to describe this moment. But one thing she didn't have much of, was time. She searched his face.

Stanley reached over for her hand, then released it. He reached over again, and Leah held it. His warmth was familiar. She wished time would stay still so they could be like this forever.

He cleared his throat. "I was looking for you," he started.

"So you said," Leah answered. When he didn't say anything, she asked, "Did you find Molly?"

A dark expression came over his face. "I did," he said.

"Oh. So, when's the wedding?"

"You heard?" He frowned. "Next week."

"I see." Disappointment filled her.

She knew it was going to happen, but hearing it...knowing it was going to be so soon, it was almost more than she could bear. Would they live in town? Would she have to pass him or Molly daily? See their happiness? Know that she was in love with Stanley, but he could never be hers?

Leah couldn't help it then. She hiccupped a sob, and said, trying to keep her voice from breaking down completely, "I hope you'll be very happy together."

"Together?" Stanley stared at her, then wiped his thumb over her cheek. "Leah, Molly and I aren't getting married."

"You—you aren't?" Leah was sure she'd heard wrong. Grief could do that to a person. She was confronting the one thing she didn't want to—Stanley and Molly—so it was obvious she was hearing wrong.

Leah took a deep breath. "I'm sorry. Can you repeat that?"

"Let me start over," Stanley said, apologetically. "Here Claudia warned me not to mess up, and I've already done that."

His comment made Leah smile, and she turned her body toward him slightly.

"See, I sent a message to Molly when we got here, like I promised. There were directions to their place waiting for me. So, I went out there."

At her nod, he continued, "But Molly...well, she wasn't welcoming at all. Not a smile or a hello. Her father was there, asked if Molly had told me. That's when I knew something was going on. Well, he went on to tell me how Molly had all kinds of men interested in her, and she'd chosen one to marry. And it wasn't me."

Leah's jaw dropped, and fury burned through her. "Do you mean to tell me, all this time you were faithful and true to Molly and she abandoned you? Because she couldn't wait just a few days more?"

"Seems like it," Stanley said. Then he grinned and stroked her cheek. "But you know what?"

"What?" Leah was curious.

Stanley took her hands in his again. "That means that I'm not getting married to her."

Leah blinked. She knew that. Why was he— "Oh!" she gasped suddenly. "Do you mean..." She bit her lip. It was too much to hope for, she wouldn't even let herself finish that thought.

"Yep," Stanley grinned. "I mean, I'm all yours, if you'll have me. I'm telling the truth, Leah, when I tell you I don't want anything more than you in my life. I'm not sure when it happened, but I fell in love with you, and I'd like to make you my wife, proper like."

He raised her hands to his lips and kissed them. Leah couldn't help but sigh in happiness. It felt so wonderful to be here with him again. She smiled at him. Everything felt right. Complete.

Except...he was frowning. Why?

"Leah," he asked, his brow furrowed. "You're making me nervous."

"Nervous? Why?" she asked.

"Because I'm asking if I can marry you. And you're just looking at me." Stanley took a deep breath, "I understand if—"

Leah stopped him with her lips on his. "Yes, Stanley Keith," she whispered. "I'd love to marry you."

Epilogue

"To the couple!"

Cheers rippled through the crowd at the wedding feast Claudia had put together for Stanley and Leah outside the town church, and Leah couldn't help but giggle in excitement. It had been a wonderful day. In fact, a wonderful week.

They'd arrived in Oregon, she'd gotten a job she enjoyed, Stanley wasn't marrying Molly, he married her, and the two of them had been making plans for the future.

At first, getting married so quickly concerned her, but Claudia had asked why she wanted to wait. Then she teased that waiting two days was still waiting longer than the first time she and Stanley had married.

Louis and Ellie were surprised but delighted, and had promised that she could continue to work there at the store, which greatly pleased Leah.

Really, nothing could make her happier than she felt right now.

Stanley sat down next to her with a plate filled with sandwiches. He set down a second one with three types of pie. "Need another drink?" he asked.

"No, I'm fine, thank you," Leah said, picking up one of the sandwiches. She looked around at the town. "Isn't it wonderful how even though we don't know too many people yet, they've all come out to celebrate with us?"

"It sure is," he agreed, picking up a slice of pie. He set it down just as quickly. "Oh! I have a surprise to tell you about."

"What's that?" she asked.

"This morning, I went out to the land office," Stanley said. "Staked out claim."

"That's wonderful. Where will we be? Oh, I do hope it's near Claudia," Leah said hopefully.

"Carl went with me. And then we drew up some plans," Stanley said. He pulled a piece of paper from his pocket, unfolded it, and showed her.

Leah looked at what she assumed were two parcels of land outlined on a small map. Within the boundaries were two small squares not too far apart. She looked at him. "I don't understand."

"These," Stanley said, pointing to the outlines, "are the claims. Yours and mine, and Carl and Claudia's." At her nod he continued, "And right here, these squares? That's where Carl and I are building houses. Right near each other, so you and Claudia can be close by."

"Oh!" Leah gasped, and threw her arms around Stanley. "This is the best gift I could have ever asked for."

"Going to take a while to get the houses built," Stanley said. "I'm hiring a few men to help, but we need to get theirs done first, seeing as they have little ones."

"Of course," Leah agreed. She clasped her hands together. "This is wonderful. Thank you, Stanley."

"It's not too far from town, so you can walk or we can take a wagon so you can get to work each day," he continued.

"Leah!"

She looked up as Claudia rushed over. "Carl just told me," she gasped. "We're going to be neighbors!"

Leah jumped up and hugged her friend. "Isn't it wonderful?" she said. "I'm so happy."

Stanley wrapped an arm around her and Leah leaned into him. "I'm so happy right now," she said, "I'm about to burst. There's only one more thing that I want."

He grinned then, a smile so big it nearly split his face in half. Leah was sure hers looked much the same. "What is it?" he asked. "If I can do it, I will."

"Oh you can do it," Leah agreed. "It's making me a promise."

"Of course. I'll do anything."

"Anything?" Leah crossed her arms and raised an eyebrow.

"Yes." Stanley looked concerned. "Just tell me what you want me to do. I want to make you happy every day for the rest of your life. That's all I want."

Leah smiled. "I just want to be with you forever. Don't ever leave me again. But if you do want to go somewhere else, then please don't ever make me walk the Oregon Trail again. I don't think my feet will ever recover."

"Nope," Stanley said. "This is where we are staying. You, me, and..." he winked at her then, "hopefully a passel of little ones to call our own."

Carl walked past then, the baby crying in his arms. "Start with this one," he grunted, clearly exhausted.

Leah giggled as Stanley took the baby and jiggled it. "I'm much better with the older ones," he said apologetically, as Claudia rushed over and took the crying child.

"The kids have had enough candy today," Claudia warned him, as she saw his hand go into his pocket.

It was too late, and the Jenkins children, along with all of the others nearby, crowded Stanley with huge grins and wide eyes.

Leah burst into a fit of giggles. "Look! Just what you wanted," she teased. "A passel of little ones."

He groaned, surrendering the sweets in his pocket to the mob of children, who thanked him and ran away. "Almost didn't survive," Stanley said, pretending to stumble toward her. "Worse than a pack of coyotes."

"Don't worry," Leah said, resting her head on his shoulder. "I'll protect you, just like you did me."

He looked down at her, and Leah couldn't help but shiver. Her heart was bursting with joy. "I'll always protect you," he said. "I love you, Leah. You're the only one for me."

She knew it was true. "I love you, Stanley."

Note from Author

Thank you for taking the time to read A Journey for Leah.

Could I ask for one small favor? Reviews like yours on Amazon mean so much to me and help others to find my books! Even just a single line means a lot!

Also...

Want a FREE book?

Stop by my website to get your no strings attached **FREE book**. It's my gift to you, as a thank you for reading this one.

www.sarahlambbooks.com

Want more?

If you enjoyed the story of Leah and Stanley, you might also like to meet Rose and Levi.

Rose and Levi only have one rule—make their own rules.

Free spirited Rose Alden is her father's youngest child, and his disappointment. Her sharp mind and wit are matched only by her sarcastic tongue and disobedience in finding a suitable husband like her older sisters did. She's desperate to live her own life, make her own rules, and marriage is not something she is interested in.

Ranch hand Levi Patterson understands just how Rose feels. It's why he's grateful to be working for her father on the Alden's quiet ranch. However, the past he thought he'd left behind has caught up, demanding he choose between the needs of others and his own.

A sudden change of events forces them each to make a decision that will change the future forever. Will Rose fight for what she longs for? Can Levi return to what was, or will he continue to blaze his own path with Rose by his side?

Find it here:

https://www.amazon.com/Romancing-Wrangler-Second-Chance-Groom-ebook/dp/B0CFWJB2W4

About the Author

Sarah is wife to an amazing teacher and mom to two boys who are growing up just a little too fast. Her day job is helping others to become writers, while she squeezes in each spare moment she can on her own books. She spends her days working and writing in the Blue Ridge Mountains and planning her next trip to Disney World.

Want more books by Sarah?

Find them all on Amazon!

https://www.amazon.com/stores/Sarah-Lamb/author/B098H3SGLK

There are other great books in this series as well!

Find all the Reluctant Wagon Train Bride books by other authors on Amazon!

https://www.amazon.com/dp/B0CDLG11HY